none

gaurav sharma presents

# of a

a collection of short stories

kind

various authors
editor: gaurav sharma

Think Tank™
Books

First published in 2020 by Think Tank Books™, New Delhi
Website: thinktankbooks.com
Email: editorial@thinktankbooks.com

Contributors assert the moral right to be identified as the authors of their stories published in the book.

This is a work of fiction. Names, characters, places and incidents are either the product of the author's imagination or are used fictitiously, and any resemblance to any actual persons, living or dead, events or locales, is entirely coincidental.

ISBN: 978-81-943705-1-2
Price: INR 225/-
Maximum retail price of this book listed is only for the Indian subcontinent. Selling price may vary elsewhere.

10 9 8 7 6 5 4 3 2 1

~~~about the editor~~~

Gaurav Sharma is the bestselling author of *The Sullied Warrior Duology*, a series of two books titled, *God of the Sullied* and *Long Live the Sullied*. He is the publisher at Think Tank Books, a Delhi-based publishing house.

Gaurav studied business at Langara College, Vancouver and journalism at GGSIP University, New Delhi. He likes playing chess and PlayStation video games.

His attempt of cohesively blending in different stories weaved by a diverse pool of authors created this 'none of a kind' book.

To know more about him, reach out via his website authorgauravsharma.com or find him on the web.

Feedback and suggestions about this book can be sent at editorial@thinktankbooks.com

~~~contents~~~

- *about the editor* — III
1. the mystical break-in | ravi dhar — 7-11
2. the value of a claddagh | shagun marwah — 12-25
3. we hit the jackpot! | shagun marwah — 26-42
4. the brutality of reality | lovey chaudhary — 43-51
5. teeth in love | tapas chanda — 52-58
6. the letter | sriraka mazumder — 59-62
7. riju | sriraka mazumder — 63-68
8. the answer | sriraka mazumder — 69-72
9. blind luck | enakshi johri — 73-79
10. cafuné | jhelum biswas bose — 80-89
11. petrichor | jhelum biswas bose — 90-101
12. saudade | jhelum biswas bose — 102-111
13. vibhatsu – the deathly fear | hasina saiyeda — 112-123
14. the last leaf | sukriti malik — 124-133
15. troubled | suchismita ghoshal — 134-141
16. so what?| amitabh srivastava — 142-150
17. trice of incubus | sulay kumar chanda — 151-155
18. amyra's first love | divya jain — 156-166
19. living the dream | richa rudra — 167-174
20. is it superstition or reality? | garima batra — 175-183
- *know more about authors* — 185-199
- *acknowledgements* — CC

~~~the mystical break-in~~~

A cluster of housing society condominiums, crisscrossed with straight perpendicular roads, lined with leafless trees, pointing their tundra-branches up to the sky, as if praying, no begging, for life-giving support from the Gods in Heaven eclipsed by the chimney smoke of poison spewing factories, while gangs of hep boys and girls zip past in swanky cars, blaring Metallica and honking horns to clear the way.

Rhea turned away from the window. There was nothing to inspire hope in the scene outside. To the contrary, it was depressing. She slammed shut the windows lest the dreariness outside should curl in with the poisonous breeze.

As she turned away from the window, she froze in fear. The door was ajar. Someone had opened the door. But how? She had bolted it from within. There was no way anyone could open that door unless someone from within would open it. She glanced around the room for any sign of an intruder. There was none.

She rushed to the door to shut it. As she pushed the door to close it, she felt powerless to do so. The door wouldn't close. She mustered all her energies to shut the door. But, it seemed to have acquired a force of its own. It resisted her with as much power as she applied. Fear sent shockwaves through her.

Rhea lived with her ailing father and her baby son. Her husband worked in Innsbruck, Austria. The money he remitted was good enough to afford the best facilities in a metropolitan city like Delhi. She lived in a high-security apartment, with round the clock security. No intruder could get into the Society apartments. Yet, there had been a break-in.

Her first impulse was to call up the Security. Then, she decided against it. She must first ascertain the well-being of her father and her baby boy. Whosoever had broken in must be somewhere here. And there was no knowing what he might be up to.

She rushed to her father's room which was the first to come in the corridor. She opened the door furtively, wishing to surprise the intruder if he was there. As the door gave way, she could see her father sleeping blissfully. She had never seen her father in so blissful a state ever since he had taken to bed.

Rhea had a brother who had left home one night after there had been a fierce altercation between father and son. When the family got to know of his disappearance in the morning, her father mounted a massive search operation, as he was himself a police officer. Days passed by into weeks, weeks into months and months into a year, but not a trace of him could be found. In the beginning, there were a few false spottings of a person by his description. But, all these were false alarms.

The shock of his disappearance killed her mother and made her father a mental and physical wreck. Her father considered himself responsible for his son's disappearance. He had been much too harsh on the boy. He had forgotten the difference between a third-degree torture room at the police station and his home. Ever since he had got bedridden. Often in his reveries, he would see the apparition of his son, and he would blabber, 'Rakesh, Rakesh, Rakesh, don't go son. See, I have paid enough for my indiscretion. Stay, please stay, your father needs you.'

Rhea would have to bring him back to reality. 'Papa, there is no one in here.' 'No, he is there', he would say, adding, 'Can't you see? For God's sake, stop him.' Rhea would lose her cool and would have to shake his father by his arm to make him see reason. And when he would keep going on, she would scream, 'Papa, please stop. There is no one here. Rakesh is gone. Never to come back. But, you please come back to your senses.' With these words, she would collapse sobbing and whimpering, because she could not see her father in that state.

The blissful look on his father's face cheered up Rhea a little. And as she made for the door to go and take a look at her baby boy, she heard her father mumble, "Rhea, is it you?" "Yes, Papa, it is me," she said. "Did you meet your brother?" "Papa, no, not again. And that too now, please." Saying so, she wanted to turn away, when her eyes fell on a bunch of freshly plucked roses beautifully wrapped into a bouquet, lying on the table. She didn't remember to have brought the roses. In fact, she never did. It was… all on a sudden, Rhea felt dazed. It was Rakesh who was fond of roses. He would always get them in the morning and place them in the vase on his study table.

Oh, God! What was happening? Was she going crazy too? No God, please don't make me lose my senses. What will happen to my baby if I lose my mind? As she pondered over these questions, her father smiled, "Go and meet your brother. He is back. He is fine. And the good thing is, he has no memory of the fight. He is changed, no doubt. Very caring and very loving. Look at those roses. He brought these for me."

Rhea thought her head was going to spin. She collected herself. She couldn't afford to become delusional. It must be some very devious person who was playing these tricks upon them. She must protect her family from this evil wizard. Her maternal instincts welled up within to fortify her against this unknown trickster.

She dashed away to her son's room. No sooner had she reached near the door than she could hear a familiar voice. She stopped. Her heart fluttered like a thousand wings. This was Rakesh. No, no, no. It could not be. Even if he were alive, how could he locate them? And what about the entry door? It was some very dangerous wizard of a man impersonating her brother.

She peered into the room stealthily. Right beside her baby was a man with his back to her. He had the same aspect as her brother's. She first thought of walking up to this man and confronting him. But, out of concern for her baby, she rushed out and called up Security to report a break-in. The security team was perplexed. No stranger, they protested, had been admitted into the Society. But, as she was complaining, a crack team was on its way to nab the person. Having secured this assurance, she made for her son's room.

As she peeped into the room, she found her baby alone in the room, with a vermillion mark on his forehead and a rudraksha necklace around his neck. Rhea's head swam in circles. Who had given this rudraksha necklace to her baby and who had applied the vermillion mark on his forehead? Innumerable unanswered questions assailed her. She struggled to find answers to them.

Right then, the bell rang. Rhea shouted, "The door is open. Get in." The bell rang again. Rhea was furious. She marched out with the baby in her lap. What she saw stupefied her. The door was closed. There was no sign of a break-in.

"Good morning, Madam! Tell us, what has happened?"

Rhea apologized for the trouble she had given them, cooking up a story of how she had forgotten to close the door and mistook it for a break-in.

~~~the value of a claddagh~~~

"I'm the unluckiest p-p-person in the whole world, Mummy. Nobody likes m-m-me," my 7-year-old stuttered while weeping, trying to keep up with the unstoppable surge of tears that ushered from her beautiful, brown little eyes. It had been barely five minutes since she entered home, threw her backpack on the floor and ran towards me.

At first, she didn't say anything. She encircled my waist with her arms and buried her face into the ruffles of my sari. She held me so tight as though she knew if I let go, she wouldn't be able to control the emotions exploding within her like a little volcano. A few moments later, that's precisely what happened. As I pressed her face between my palms, settling her soft, goldilocks-like curls behind her ears, she looked at me with a set of eyes that didn't wish to reveal the pain they felt or the thoughts that clouded her mind. But it was too late, and I already knew what had happened. Well, most of it.

"Losing one competition doesn't matter, honey. Learn from it, and you will win next time," I tried to console, but as the first tear broke free and rolled down her cheek, the rest just followed it in a stream. Since then, she tried to tell me, in bits and pieces, the accounts of the 'worst day in her life'. I noticed how every now and then, she also tried to wipe off her tears on the cuffed sleeves of her uniform just so that I wouldn't have to bend forward and keep doing it for her every second. She was already, so brave.

"Darling, just because they tell you that you can't do it, doesn't mean that you shouldn't."

"But m-maybe, they're r-right, Mumma. Maybe, I can't. Just because I l-love doing something, doesn't mean that I'll ever be good at it. I'm just f-f-fooling myself," she confessed. While her mind was starting to accept it, her heart continued to break.

"Sweetheart, you don't have to do things perfectly to do them 'well'. You will get endless opportunities to try again. This was just one stepping stone along the way. Do you hear me?" I kissed her cushiony cheek, wet with tears so that she wouldn't have to feel them again. If only I could kiss away all her little droplets of worries the same way.

"But I couldn't s-top s-tuttering, and they couldn't stop l-laughing. Nobody even heard my p-poem. I had worked so hard! I will never do this again. Never, ever again!" she declared, burying her face into the furry, soft toys that were placed along the bedside.

"Okay, sweetie. If you don't want to do it again, no one will force you. At the end of the day, it's your talent, and you get to choose what you want to do with it." I announced in a gentle yet matter-of-fact tone, trying to make her admit what she really wanted to do.

It so worked for she slowly stood up from the bed and looked at me in a way that usually corrects me if I'm wrong. Her expressions could tell how shocked she was.

"But you and Dadda always told me that I should n-ever q-quit, come what may," she confirmed with furrowed eyebrows, wiping her leftover tears on both the cheeks.

"I know. But you seem so confident that you won't be able to do this again. You don't even want to try doing it even if you know you can. So, what's the point?"

"But... I'm just... s-s-cared. What if I start s-s-stammering while reciting my poems again? What if they tease me again?" she revealed, sadly. I could feel her helplessness growing. After all, being born with a speech defect wasn't her fault, was it?

"Then, my love, you will continue reciting what you wrote and finish what you started."

"It's not that easy! As soon as they start l-l-laughing, I lose my f-focus, Mummy."

"Then, you'll just have to learn to ignore it. People only laugh because they see something in you which they don't see in themselves. A talent, a passion, a potential. They will want to pull you down as much as possible so that you lose your focus and then, your confidence. That's the only way it'll keep you from winning!" I clarified.

"But how do I stay c-confident despite what they say? Will, anyone, ever l-love me for who I am - the way you do? Or, will I have to ignore everyone... f-f-forever?"

I must admit. Her questions did give me a Deja-vu, almost leaving me speechless. It wasn't too long ago when I posed the very same questions to my mother while crying my eyes out, hoping to hear something that might change my life.

That's when I knew. It was time to tell her the story of a Claddagh.

I convinced her to lay that cute little head onto my lap as I fell back to the support of the bed and snuggled under the covers. I assured her that it would be fine if she fell asleep this way too, for she deserved this rest more than anyone else. But boy, did she love hearing my stories with full concentration! As I saw her eyes widening with a twinkle of curiosity, something told me that this little girl wouldn't be dosing off too soon.

"Okay, darling. I'm going to tell you a story that will answer all your questions in a jiffy. Remember, this story has special powers. It can guide you and stay with you forever, depending on what you learn from it. So, you have to listen to it very carefully and with a big smile on your face. That's the only way you get to receive a special prize in the end!"

"What special prize??" she asked with her lips slowly, beginning to curve into a smile.

"That's a surprise, my love. You will have to wait for it. So, do you promise?"

"Yes yes, I promise, Mommy!" she asserted, with a joyful grin. I was glad this was already making her feel better. How much we underestimate the magic of words!

"Once upon a time, there was an old, retired couple who loved each other very much but every so often, struggled to make their ends meet. Irrespective of how hard they worked, they couldn't keep up with the evergrowing expenses of the city and soon, ran out of every last bit of their hard-earned savings. They didn't want to inform their only son about this condition for they knew he'd do anything in his ability to provide his parents with utmost comfort, even if that included sacrificing his own family's needs.

So, they stayed silent and tried to live with as minimum necessities as possible. They never spoke of the troubles but only of their sweet love which only made them strong enough to deal with every crisis that emerged. They knew that if someday, something terrible were to happen, they would be okay as long as they had each other to hold and protect. Little did they know, a tragedy was almost on its way.

One day, the husband was struck with pneumonia. They had been running out of medicines, food and milk for a while too, but never once did he complain. He had made himself content with as much warm milk and dates as he could eat every day. Most of the times, even the wife would quietly add her share of food to his plate so that he would have more energy to fight. She would then weep hungrily to sleep, knowing that if she didn't do anything soon, she would lose her best friend and her only strength in life.

She had no other choice but to sell the most prized possession of her marriage - a gorgeous ring with which her husband had proposed to her some 50 years ago. It was also the last piece of jewellery that she had owned and saved, letting all the others go as quickly as they were acquired during their initial days of richness.

However, this ring posed more hesitancy than admiration. You see, this ring was incredibly unique. It was embellished with an exquisite, heart-shaped diamond in the middle, clasped together with two hands on both sides and a sparkling crown on top. No person had until then, witnessed a design that rare. Surprising as it was, the ring didn't seem to fit in with anyone's expectations. They all wanted the same old traditional gold or silver bands studded with flowers, diamonds, or expensive jewels.

Knowing that it was the only way to save her husband's life, she did not stop trying, nevertheless. Even during the coldest winter the city had ever witnessed, she travelled door-to-door, one neighbourhood to another, in search of that one person whom she longed to sell her ring for a handsome price. Much to her despair, several weeks had passed, but not a single soul had shown her kindness. Even the blue-red frostbites on her toes didn't seem to hurt as badly as the broken pieces of her aching heart.

One evening, as she travelled through a dim-lit lane on her way back home, she noticed a faint flicker of light gleaming through the windows of some house at the end of the street. She couldn't remember paying a visit to that one for it may have seemed abandoned or quieter when she passed through it earlier. Hence, she decided to give it a chance, knowing very well in her heart that it might have been her last.

When she pushed the door open of this charming little wooden house, she found herself taken aback by the spellbinding beauty of what lay inside. It was almost like magic. While rows of gold and silver, diamonds, rubies, sapphires and various other jewels adorned the bricked walls, the neatly-arranged glass tables with thousands of rings and necklaces led to a mesmerizing reflection that shined from every nook and cranny. That's when it hit her. It wasn't just somebody's house; it was a jewel merchant's shop.

A few moments later, she was welcomed by a humble man who's smile seemed brighter than all his jewels combined. Since the woman had loved wearing and repurchasing different kinds of jewellery when she was younger and richer, she couldn't help notice a few of her favourites among his creations and talked to him about the designs that she particularly liked and why. Impressed by her excellent taste and eye for detail, he offered her to sit and try some on too. Sensing the quiet hesitation, he tried to make her feel more welcomed. He quickly prepped up a delicious cup of coffee with a plate full of almond biscottis. He even lit the fireplace with fresh coal for a warmer ambience.

For the woman, this was no less than a dream. The man was so kind that he had almost made her forget her worries. But soon enough, she was brought back to reality. She finally confessed to him the real reason for her visit. Then, carefully, she took the ring out of her bag and unclothed the enchanting beauty on the glass table in front of him.

"Whom did you buy this from?" he asked, trying to justify his shocked expression.

"My husband gifted it to me on the day of our marriage. His great-grandmother had saved it for years and passed it down through generations," the woman replied.

"And you want to sell this? For money? My dear, do you know how much this is worth?"

"I'm assuming not much. Nobody from this city or the neighbouring villages have been interested in buying it. Not even for 5-10 gold coins," the woman stated, sadly.

"Well, I'm not surprised. You were trying to sell it to all the wrong people. Don't you know? They are clones. They only want what the majority of people seek. It's rare to find someone real in today's world. As real as this ring. No wonder you were seeking its value in all the wrong places. Only an expert could recognize the true worth of a ring as precious as this. If I were you, I wouldn't sell it even for 50 coins," he announced.

At first, the woman couldn't believe what she was hearing.

"But, why?" were the only words that could come out of her mouth, for now.

"Because, my dear, this is not just any ordinary ring. It is a Claddagh, a traditional Irish ring that first originated in the 17th Century. Craftsmen don't make such rings anymore, and if they do, they are out of the reach of any layman. As it should be, for this ring holds a special significance that very few understand..." he resumed,

"... Do you see these three symbols - the heart, the hands and the crown? They symbolize the three core values of every relationship - Love, Loyalty and Friendship. The precious heart in the middle signifies the unconditional love that two people feel for each other; the two hands on each side, holding onto the love within, represent the promise of friendship and the power of never letting go of each other. And the crown on top of the heart represents the loyalty that lays the foundation of an everlasting connection. Together, these three symbols represent a bond of love that goes above and beyond what average couples may feel for each other, today..." he continued, "So, if your husband gifted this to you, I must say, you are an incredibly lucky woman!"

Hearing the same, she was choked in tears. Despite having owned this ring for more than five decades, she had failed to understand what it truly meant. She did feel like the luckiest woman in the world today, for this ring had perfectly described her marriage of 50 years. Suddenly, she felt a sense of attachment towards it. She didn't want to sell it any longer. She wanted to wear it on her finger until her last breath. But the thought of seeing her husband die wasn't something she was ready to digest as well. Suddenly, she had an idea for which all she needed was a wee bit of the sweet man's help.

Soon enough, the woman returned home to her husband whom she had found sleeping, next to two large bowls full of milk and dates which had now gotten cold and soggy. She realized that he must have dozed off while waiting for her, as always. She then quietly replaced the old, worn-out blanket with a new, cosier one that she had just bought from the market, and lit the fireplace with enough lumps of coal to last a few weeks. Gently, she woke him up with a kiss, fed him the required medicines and one sip at a time, helped him devour a piping hot bowl of creamy and tangy, tomato soup - his favourite.

Upon seeing this, the man wanted to cry tears of joy and ask a million questions, but as he heard her say, "Shush, shush. I'll explain everything to you tomorrow, sweetie. For now, just enjoy this moment with me and go to sleep," all he did was smile and kiss his wife. That night, the old couple had never felt richer or more in love with each other."

"So, did you like the story, honey?" I finally asked, heaving a sigh of relief.

"No, Mummy, I didn't like it. I loved it!" she exclaimed with joy. "But I just couldn't understand one bit. What was the old woman's idea that made her richer?"

"I was waiting for you to ask that question, only. Well, since that sweet man was a jewel merchant and was always looking for new ideas and designs to take his business to new heights, she decided to let him borrow her Claddagh ring for a few days until he was able to make a replica of it. He was then the first jeweller in their city to have created and sold countless Claddagh rings from that day onwards. And for this, he paid the couple more than enough money to let them live a comfortable and happy life."

"That's amazing! I loved that merchant from the beginning. He was so k-k-kind and generous. And the couple too. They loved each other so much!" she spoke excitedly.

"I agree. But what is the most important thing that we learnt from this story?"

"That we're all unique in our own special ways, and we don't n-need to fit in with the other members of the s-society. I'm just like the c-c-Claddagh ring, and someday, I'll find my jewel merchants too who will recognize my true value," she narrated while jumping from one corner of the room to another. She usually did that when she was too happy.

"Perfect. So, now, my dear little jewel, are you ready for your final surprise?"

"Oh, yes, yes!" By the looks of it, she had seemed to forget all about it until that second.

Carefully, I took out a tiny, blue-coloured box that lay under a pile of clothes in my closet and placed it in front of her on the bed.

As she slowly opened the box, all the while keeping her eyes closed, she couldn't believe what she had finally, discovered.

It was a Claddagh ring!

She was in complete awe of its priceless beauty. So was I, every time I looked at it.

"But... but how do you have this, Mummy?" she said, staring at the one-of-a-kind ring.

"Well, it turns out that the story is based on true incidents from your great-great-grandmother's life. This ring was passed on from one generation to another from my side of the family, eventually reaching my father who in turn, gave it to my mother when they got married who then further gave it to me when I was your age and listening to this story for the first time..." I confessed, feeling proudly nostalgic.

"... So, today, I gift you this timeless Claddagh as a symbol of self-worth. Whenever you feel low or unloved, let this ring remind you that you're a gem of a person who deserves nothing but the best of everything in the world and that someday, you will be recognized for your poems which are going to be just as real and beautiful as you are. But for now, you're the most prized possession of my life, and I love you the most," I concluded.

I could feel the tears in her eyes, yet again. But this time, they were the happy ones.

"I love you more, Mumma. You will always be my Claddagh!"

~~~we hit the jackpot!~~~

"No, Sonali, no. Love stories are just not my thing!" I tried to be as stern as possible, hoping that my friend would just give up on me already.

"But you agreed to it yesterday. You can't ditch me now." Sonali declared, with her eyebrows furrowed. It was usually indicative of her annoyance.

"Listen, you know I don't like such sappy, mushy, romantic movies, don't you? I can barely read one page of a love story, let alone watch a 3-hour-long movie in a hall," I admitted.

"I know. But I already bought the tickets for us. This might be our only chance to catch up before the preparatory holidays for boards begin. I don't want to go without you, Serena. Please, come for me?" she pleaded.

"Then, why couldn't you just convince everyone to go for a horror or thriller movie, instead?" I asked with a straight face.

"I tried, but nobody wanted to watch them, except for you. Come on! It's just one movie. I'll buy you a large tub of half cheese and half caramel popcorn. Just the way you like it." She spoke with such confidence as though she knew that luring me with popcorn would work. It didn't.

"No. You go ahead with the other girls today. We'll go out next weekend," I announced.

"I don't get it. What's so wrong with watching or reading love stories, anyway?" her eyebrows were getting scarier now.

"There's nothing wrong with them. I just find the concept of 'love' that they try to preach, a bit delusional. Boy meets girl. They instantly click, fall in love, cry a thousand rivers and then, live happily ever after. How naïve do they possibly think we are?" I confessed.

"Stop being such a pessimist, Serena. At least, not today!" Naina overheard our conversation from behind and decided to budge in.

"I'm not a pessimist. I'm just practical. I don't see myself catching a stranger's eye anytime soon and realizing that he's 'the one' I have been waiting for all my life. You see hundreds of people every single day and come in contact with almost a million strangers. How do you expect to identify your particular soulmate some random day, out of the blue, and fall in love with him? Such meet-cutes are only a staple of romantic comedies." I knew I had to explain my point.

"Alright, alright. I'm leaving before this discussion kills my buzz." Naina pulled out a straightener from her bag and made her way towards the corner of the room with a plug point.

"I'm going to get ready now, and I suppose you guys should, too, if you don't want to get scolded by Sister."

She was right. It was already one, and the event was about to start in less than an hour.

"I don't know about you, but I am somehow, starting to get a little pumped up about this," Saloni decided to tease me while dabbing a baby pink blush on the apples of her cheeks.

"Listen. You better not ditch me out there. Especially, not for a boy - no matter how cute he is. Have I made myself clear?" I replied strictly.

She laughed. "Crystal. But, you know what? I have a feeling that you're going to enjoy it way more than any of us today. And deep down, I know you're pretty excited for it, too!"

She couldn't have been more wrong. All I wanted to do was dance, eat and have a good time with my girl gang. I was going to be least bothered by the presence of those boys.

Long story short, I was in a convent school. You know what they say about girls from an all-girls school, don't you? They're shy, reserved, and a bit awkward around boys. Well, if you think I was like any of them, you're wrong. I was worse. But just for a little while. This shyness and awkwardness later turned into a blatant disinterest. Sure, I had crushes, now and then, but they only seemed nice enough to be admired from a distance, like a work of art. I would casually pass a smile, listen to their conversations, laugh at their jokes, but as soon as they would expect me to talk, I would make up some stupid excuse and run. Literally. Then again, I never met any boy who was charming or smart enough to make me want to stay and interact with him.

Well, thanks to my school's weird rules, my friends thought that this was going to change today. Every year, our Headmistress organized a special event for seniors at our school, similar to what foreign schools did, especially in almost every Hollywood rom-com or chick-flick - a Prom Night. Only in our school it happened in the daytime and was called Socials. If the name wasn't obvious enough, the main aim of this party was for us to be 'social'. But no, not with each other. Instead, with the sole species of the universe whom most of our parents disliked and because of who's mere existence, we were sent to an all-girls school in the first place.

Yes. The forbidden opposite sex. Boys. Not just ordinary boys, though. Boys from an all-boys Christian school who probably had no idea what to say in front of girls too. Let that sink in.

As I entered the auditorium where Socials was about to start anytime now, I noticed the way all my classmates stood in queues of three, one behind the other. Honestly, they never looked this disciplined; must have been the nerves. They also never looked this beautiful. They're obviously going to be hard to compete with. Good thing, I didn't intend to. Suddenly, I heard Sister shout from a distance, "C'mon, you three! Move quickly!" I tried to hurry up but soon, realized that I had chosen the worst day ever to wear stilettos for the first time. The colour of these heels may have matched my dress perfectly, but my feet hurt like hell. Being stabbed with needles would have been less painful. I could barely walk without Sonali or Naina's support. I couldn't ditch them now, even if I wanted.

When we reached the corner of the room where Sister stood furiously with her arms crossed across her chest, our eyes went straight towards this huge, multicoloured bowl of chits on the table.

"You're late, young ladies. Now, pick a chit from this bowl and stand in your assigned spots. The boys will be here any second," she declared. We were all taken aback. Nobody had warned us against this game of fate. I thought we were supposed to be "social" or mingle with whoever we wanted. In our case, we had already planned to ditch our partners after some time and enjoy the party with each other. The fact that we were going to be assigned partners based on these numbers meant that we had to talk to them. We didn't have a choice anymore.

As I put my hand into the bowl, I could feel my fingers trembling through the crisp paper chits. I could feel the tension growing within my nerves. When I finally pulled one out, I was horrified. I read it out loud, "No. 180!" Wait. Does that school even have 180 boys? What if they run out of boys and I'm the only one who ends up all alone, partner-less? I'll be a joke. Why did my chance have to come so late? It seemed like a good enough reason for me to run, once again. But I had promised Sonali that I wouldn't ditch her. So, I decided to take it with a pinch of salt.

Within a few minutes, a group of well-suited boys entered our auditorium. By the looks of it, they seemed a lot more nervous than us. Some of them even looked terrified. I forgot how awkward this would have been for them as well. Then, one by one, our Headmistress called out the chit numbers, and two opposite species from two different schools came towards each other in the centre of the room and went towards their seats. If this wasn't dramatic enough, each boy had a rose which was meant to be passed onto their partners. They didn't have a choice, either.

Then, I waited for my chance. I waited and waited and waited for a while more. It had been more than 40 minutes since I was standing in those wretched heels. My friends had already been introduced to their partners by now and were comfortably seated. Finally, the moment had arrived. As soon as I heard No. 180, a shiver went down my spine. As I proceeded towards my partner, those pointy, nasty heels made me want to scream my lungs out. So much so, I almost lost my balance.

What if I trip and fall on my back in front of everyone today? I'll be teased as 'Humpty Dumpty, who had a great fall' for generations to come. As a result, I kept telling myself, "Don't fall. Don't fall. Please don't fall..." under my breath until I reached the place where he stood. I took one look at him, snatched the rose away from his hand while hearing him say, "I guess this is for you!" and ran towards our seats as quickly as possible without making it seem too obvious.

Once we settled down, I felt as though I had accomplished the biggest battle in the world. I heaved a sigh of relief and looked around. Surprisingly, everyone had started talking to their partners, much sooner than I had imagined. That's when I realized something. My battle wasn't quite over yet. It had only begun. I still had to socialize with a partner who had supposedly 'guessed' that the rose was for me. As if he was dying to get more suitable options. Huh!

I didn't say anything in the beginning. I wanted him to initiate the conversation like most of the guys did. But he remained too quiet for too long. What was he thinking? Was he still 'guessing' that he was supposed to talk to me? I tried to look at him from the corner of my eyes. I liked what I saw so far. He had a cute face. But why wasn't he smiling?

Was he upset to have me as a partner? Did he wish to be paired with someone more beautiful? I caught a glimpse of his glasses. He looked like the studious kind; a sweet, obedient kid. But almost like an enigma, broody and mysterious, if that made any sense. Surprising as it was, I felt a sudden need from within to get to know him better - or at least, hear his voice a little. So, I continued to wait.

Pretty soon, I found myself getting bored. I must have yawned a few times too. I envied my friends who even from a distance, seemed to be getting along with their partners quite well. Suddenly, I don't know what came onto me. Before I could even think, I opened my mouth, and the only words that came out of it were, "So, were you guys forced to wear suits? Or was it a personal choice?" I hoped that he would reply with at least some enthusiasm or energy.

"No no, it was a dress code. Brother would have sent us right back home if we disobeyed him. But it makes sense. Otherwise, half of the guys in my class would have arrived in pyjamas or boxers," he answered with an innocent grin.

So, he does speak and has a lovely voice. Bonus - He has a good sense of humour too.

"I know what you mean. If it weren't for our dress code, we would have all come in jeans and t-shirts too," I responded in a similar tone.

"Really? I was assuming that a dress would have been a personal choice for all of you. Don't most girls like wearing dresses to parties or events like these?" he asked curiously.

"Well, yes, but then most of the girls don't realize the risk of wearing such dresses at a party. You're supposed to have fun, which means that you should be able to eat or do whatever you want without constantly worrying about spoiling it. Plus, if you're wearing a nice dress, you're most likely to pair it up with equally nice, sky-high heels. Especially the ones in which you can barely move, let alone dance like crazy." The realization of not being able to dance finally struck me, and he almost caught me looking down sadly at my feet.

"Is that the reason why you ran as soon as you took the rose from me? You can't walk properly too, can you?" He asked in such a sweet and considerate manner that it almost made him sound smart without making me feel dumb. I didn't realize that was possible.

"So, you caught that, huh? Yeah, I was trying to sit before I fell and hurt myself - or worse, someone else," I said, shyly.

"Don't worry. I wouldn't have let you fall. That's why I tried to stay right behind you, even though it was a bit tough to catch up with you…" Wait. Did he just flirt? Is that how subtly it's done?

"…But I must admit something. This is better than what I had in mind. I almost thought you were trying to run away from me," he continued, mischievously.

"No, no. I'm pretty sure that would be you in some time," I laughed.

"We'll see about that," he winked.

If only I knew how terribly wrong he was at that point.

"So, I suppose, your name is Serena?" he asked, finally.

"Yes, how did you know?" I looked puzzled.

"One of your teachers told me when they called out the chit number and saw you walk across the hall towards me."

"Oh, okay!"

"My name is Aman. Just saying!" He said, after a slight pause.

Shoot. I was supposed to ask his name. Say something back now. Anything.

"Nice." Wait a second. Nice? Did I just compliment his name? I felt like kicking myself in the gut.

"So, what do you think the show will be about?" He broke the awkward silence once again.

"I think a few girls from my class will do stand-up comedy. Some might sing and dance, too."

"Will you do something?" He asked eagerly. I almost saw a twinkle in his eyes.

"No way! I can't bear the thought of having so many people look at me. I'll either end up barfing or fainting on the stage out of anxiety."

"Really? But you seem so confident to me," he expressed, without an iota of doubt.

"Not really! I mean, I'm only confident around my friends. I take a lot of time to open up."

"Then, I'm glad we're friends already!" He smirked.

His smile - oh, boy, that smile! I knew I was going to have a hard time forgetting it.

It had been 15 minutes since the show had begun, but surprisingly, we couldn't stop talking. We observed each performance keenly, discussed what we liked or didn't like and laughed most of the time. At one point, I even saw one of the teachers look back to figure out who had been talking non-stop. We didn't care.

We were doing exactly what they wanted us to do, after all. We were being 'social'.

The show ended in the blink of an eye. Even then, we continued to talk. There was not a single moment when I felt bored or exhausted. I just couldn't get enough of him. It was unbelievable how incredibly in-sync we were. I saw Sonali, staring at me in awe from a distance. She was just as happy and shocked as I was. Then, I saw Naina signalling me to come out for lunch.

Before I could say another word, he gently asked, "So, are you on Facebook?"

At that time, this question was equivalent to being asked for your number. I wish he did, though, but for now, I was happy with my share of butterflies in the tummy. Nevertheless, I tried to stay as calm as possible without revealing a flicker of excitement on my face. All I did was smile.

"Of course. Only I'm not too active. So, you won't be able to find me easily," I answered.

"Don't worry! I'll figure a way out. See you soon," he said sweetly. Then, without even giving me a chance to respond, he got up and left the auditorium. I assumed that he went to meet his friends too.

As soon as he left, my friends came running from behind and pulled me towards the lunch table, where half of the food was already over. I didn't care. I was too ecstatic to eat. I told them all about him - what a sweetheart he was, his great sense of humour, and how we clicked within seconds. I was dying to introduce him to my girls and meet his friends too. There was so much more I wanted to talk about and know if he was maybe, open to the idea of dancing with me too.

Unfortunately, all my plans came crashing down. I kept waiting for Aman to return after our lunch break, but somehow, he went weirdly missing. My friends and I searched for him everywhere - across the hall, outside the auditorium, around the campus. At first, I thought that he might have gotten lost. Our buildings could be a bit confusing for someone new. But all efforts went in vain. None of his batch mates had seen him too.

Was he even real, or did I just imagine him all along? Or was it a weird dream that I had to wake up from? It was then when I realized how guys must have felt when I'd run away from them too. So, was Karma trying to teach me a lesson? Was I getting a taste of my own medicine?

Just then, I heard some of the guys say that they noticed Aman leave a few minutes ago without informing anyone. Why did he leave so soon? Was he okay? Was there an emergency? I had no option but to wait and wonder. Later, I decided to go to the movie with the girls just to take my mind off him. But every love story or meet-cute now ended up reminding me of him. And how my life had played this cruel joke with me by giving me something so beautiful to believe in and then, taking it away from me, without giving me a chance to comprehend it completely.

I was still desperate to get all my answers. So, I waited for Aman's Facebook request for weeks. He never sent one. When I tried looking him up online, I couldn't find a single Aman from that school who looked even remotely like him. After a few months, I lost all hope. Our board exams were approaching, and I couldn't bear the risk of falling behind for someone who ceased to exist. Soon, he became this wonderful memory I quietly recalled for years, with a hope that somewhere, someday, I'll meet someone like him and click, once again.

Little did I know, destiny had a different plan saved up for me.

Five years later, I was tagged in an old school picture by one of my classmates on Instagram. The image was from Naina's 18th birthday, right after we had danced round-the-clock for hours. My hair was messy and frizzy, my kajal had smudged due to excessive sweating, and my teeth looked enormously big and scary. The memories might have been sweet, but the picture was pure evil. I had to untag myself as soon as possible.

But I might have been an hour or two late. Someone I knew, already saw it and I could no longer escape the consequences of it.

Before I could ping the nasty friend who tagged me in that terrible picture, I received a personal message from someone called Aman Mehra. The name didn't ring any bell at first. I was least bothered. I knew way too many people by this first name to let it affect me anyway. So, I casually opened his message which read,

"Hey, are you the same girl in the pink dress whom I met at Socials a few years ago? If not, I'm sorry to bother you - whoever you are. If yes, I'm sorry it took me so long to find you."

My heart started pounding so fast that I could almost hear it through my chest. My mind became numb, my hands were quivering, and my cheeks flushed a bright, red colour, that very second.

Could it be him? After all these years? Or was somebody playing a mean trick with me again?

That's when it hit me. In the tagged photo, I was wearing the same pink dress on Naina's birthday as I was on the day of Socials. It was the last day I wore it, for I had spilt orange juice all over it; I should have practised what I preached. But how did he recognize me this perfectly?

Before I could gather enough courage to respond, I checked his profile to be 100% sure.

Ah! There he was. That adorable, innocent-looking face. That mischievous, twinkle in his eyes. Those heart-shaped lips, forming an attractive little smile. I couldn't stop staring at his images.

I suddenly remembered every little detail of that event like it only happened yesterday, and with that came flashbacks of the most amazing memories, with an inevitable amount of anger too.

"Hey, mystery guy. I'll forgive you as long as you promise to answer all my questions honestly, without disappearing on me again." I wrote back, realizing I was still a little mad at him.

It didn't last long, though. I couldn't resist smiling from ear to ear when I read his next message,

'NEVER! <3'

After dating for four years and being married for seven, I can safely say that he has kept his promise and hasn't run away from me since then. Not yet, at least. He also brings me roses every so often to compensate for what he said on the day we met.

'I guess' he still doesn't have a choice, does he?

The best part is that every time our daughter questions the power of fate or the presence of true love in the world, he never gets tired of reminding her, "Did you know that I won your mom in a lottery, honey? She is the best prize I ever received in my life, and one day, you will win too. Destiny may work in the most unexpected ways, but it's always worth the wait in the end."

That's how I knew - we hit the jackpot!

~~~the brutality of reality~~~

"Revenge is a dish best served cold," said Don Corleone in 'The Godfather' on TV while we were back home winding down and recovering from the dinner at Raghu's house.

My handsome father was wearing his most expensive and favourite red tie for dinner planned at his would-be son in law's house. He towered over me, but the wide grin on his face instantly made me feel at ease. We listened to and sang along with R.D Burman and Rafi songs while driving to their house, but to our surprise, Raghu's mother, Shefali, was already a couple of whiskeys down when we landed at their door, and, on a binge, to say whatever was on her mind. The highlight of the meetup was Shefali calling me a 'bitch' in her slurred speech which sounded more like a 'witch'. I was called names to marry her only beloved son, and to take him 'away' from her. By talking to my father about politics and religion, Raghu 's father, Kulbhushan, was tirelessly trying to neutralize the situation at the table.

I was dressed traditionally in a pretty salwar kameez suit, with an exquisitely embroidered floral dupatta. My chaperoning brother made a place for me on the sofa. I was meeting Raghu for the first time. He worked as an IT engineer in a reputed company in Gurgaon. It was an arranged marriage set up. My grandfather knew his family, and on an auspicious date, they wanted to get us married. I had just turned 18 this year. He was 19.

My little brother, Melvin was so angry with the new relatives that he didn't even eat his favourites, red sauce pasta, and chicken wings at the dinner table. My father was generous and told us to be respectful and kind towards everyone. He had always been caring towards us to compensate for the absence of my mother.

On the way home, I also learned that naive Melvin was about to throw a glass bowl at Shefali to poke a hole in her head. He whispered it into my ears so our father can't hear. I giggled with Melvin and felt so blessed that I had such a perfect family around me.

To me, the entire situation has been very conventional and flimsy where the mother-in-law is stereotypically judgmental, hates the daughter-in-law, and fears losing control of her family.

I had hoped, Raghu and I will fall head over heels in love with each other after marriage. Marriage is, after all, a vow to be with one another forever. I had plans to be a doctor as a little girl but let bygones be bygones.

I thought we are meant to be. I could just stare at him for hours. I couldn't get him out of my head. I daydreamed about him and us being together. I had fallen in love with him, and that's all that mattered.

The following weekend, we had a small ceremony at Raghu's home. I expected to meet Shefali in a sober state this time. Shefali's laugh echoed as we entered the house. It is Disney creepy, like a witch peeping her head into the enchanted cauldron to see the beaks of the hawks and the hearts of the chickens' brew as they should.

Her face was hidden inside a humidifier that sat like a stand on the coffee table. What I saw was a big plastic box that had curly, frosty hair on top. She was not ready for the ceremony. No one was prepared for the ceremony. Had we arrived ahead of schedule?

Apparently, Shefali forgot what happened last time. As she offered me food while questioning my cooking skills, she seemed perfectly normal. She shamed my body with constant derisions. She told me to keep my food rationed until the wedding. She was also very keen to let me know that if I want to get married to her son, I must watch my weight. I weighed 48kgs.

After another three hours of chitchatting about my imperfections, everyone got ready for the ceremony, and Raghu and I were engaged. I felt scared.

The ceremony ended and Shefali spoke harshly about my weight and jawline and was back to her usual self. I think I had a jawline that could cut her into fine and equal pieces.

The father-in-law gave me a bear hug to welcome me as a daughter and member of the family as we left for our home. Melvin was in no mood for any more mockeries.

Raghu's family was so rushed about getting things done that we got married within two days.
Time went by amidst chaos and noise. We got married. Five hundred guests from around the world attended the wedding. The mathematical figure was very essential to Raghu's family.

My dad hoped that my marriage to Raghu would be a success. In reality, a lot of arranged marriages do work. I was full of excitement and apprehension.

On my first day, I was placed in a room different from Raghu's. He had not even talked to me for the many following days. I thought he was shy and timid. I did everything I could to be a part of his family. Yet he ignored me.

Shefali used to regularly watch a program on TV, where a medium helps people interact with their dead relatives. I realized she was probably more comfortable relating to the deceased than to the living. She was always her unpredictable, erratic, and cruel self. And, in the house, 'Bitch' had become a common term used for me.

At this point, she began to assault me physically and mentally. My role had been only to look after the house like a maid. And she used to make me wash her feet, and I was never left alone with my husband from the day I arrived.

When I tried to express myself to Raghu, he beat me up for talking rubbish about his mum. That was the beginning of the end for my desire to conform and stay in this marriage. My imaginary and perfect life was shattered into pieces. I withdrew into myself, painfully sad, ashamed to tell my father about it.

Why am I not as powerful as other women, I used to ask myself?

My marriage was eventually consummated after four months but it was not a satisfying physical relationship. It wasn't loving. It wasn't what I hoped for. I think the familial relationships were complicated. It's just that we were different people with baggage worth a lifetime amongst each other, everyone trying to live inside the multifarious layers of the pretence. Even so, I did not have any feeling that something was wrong then.

The way my father-in-law looked at me had changed. His eyes seemed to linger on me a little longer than usual, which made me uncomfortable. I couldn't shake the impression behind his stares; there was something sinister.

I recall an incident of the examination hall in school, once the instructor took rounds and stroked my nape softly only to shrug it off later and shame an eleven-year-old girl. I was red with shame and figured it was just my imagination. When the bushy-looking guy in the packed DTC bus ground his crotch onto my ass, I thought to myself, maybe, it's not what I think. No one would deliberately do that, could be a mistake.

Then again, in the general coach of the metro, my bra was unhooked, and I let it go because maybe, it's just in my head. The nineties were harder, and years later, the female body was always subject to the whims and fancies of men.

Being a woman, having walked through countless instances of unwanted touching by random people anywhere and everywhere, I had formed a mentality where I still felt insecure so maybe, again, this time, it's in my head.

It was Shefali's birthday, and I was waiting for a beep beep from the microwave. I baked a cake for her. Afterwards, we were scheduled to go out for dinner, but

Shefali suddenly got one of her staple headaches. I think It's her sinuses that are the problem. They're always blocked, I wonder why! I secretly love it when she experiences these headaches. They make her lose her appetite. They're so horrible at times that she doesn't move for hours. She lies on the couch, and shut her eyes and look more pained than when open. It's like she's trying to push the headache out through her forehead, like a cow pushing out her baby.

This reminds me of my childhood. I was a fluffy little baby. I blew gleaming sound bubbles. I loved the motion, the light, the colour, and the music, the textures, and the stones. For hours I would lie on the floors, feeling the coldness and patting the surface in ecstasy so hard that my hands and feet would blur. Now being all grown up, my anxiety and depression had gone off the edge.

Shefali yelled at me to bring her some painkillers to relieve the pain. I hurried to do the needful. Her shrilling voice hurt my eardrums and the glass windows. She quickly gulped down three pills to magically make the pain go away. And, off she went to sleep while listening to people on television interacting with the dead.

Raghu had not yet come from office for the birthday celebrations of his dear mother.

After running all day around the house, I went upstairs to relax. I dozed off thinking what caused a lot of strife for me is that I never knew if Raghu was genuinely incapable of understanding my point of view, or if he didn't want to comprehend.

Shockingly, I woke up to my father-in-law harassing me. He was trying to kiss me and grope me. I froze, stunned, and prayed it was going to be the end. But it was like a switch had flicked inside him, and for the first time that night, he tried to rape me brutally.

As I was struggling under his heavy body, unable to move, I was crying out for Raghu and Shefali, but no one was there to help. I pleaded for him to stop, but he was getting louder and louder, "but you like this, don't you?"

I could feel the gut-wrenching agony in my body. He tried to terrorize me into silence. He also tried to convince me that if I said anything, people would think there was something terribly wrong with me, and they would send me away forever.

He scratched my face with his sweaty palms and said, "I will make you pregnant if my son can't."

"Leave me! Please," as I cried out of lungs.

During the abuse, I felt like I had left my body and gone somewhere else in my mind because I couldn't survive the experience in any other way. I hoped it would be one-off, but it looked like he was hungry for more after striking me the very first time. Every inch of me was destroyed.

He slapped me hard and ramped up the abuse until I managed to get off and run downstairs for help. I wanted to call Raghu or just scream loud enough to wake up Shefali or the neighbours. He followed me down and threatened to kill me if I said a word. I fled into the kitchen and hid inside the shelf. Somehow, he had turned into a demon, a demon who could tear my body apart, roast it, and eat it as a side dish. I had never felt this mute and helpless before. There was the world out there, but I wasn't part of it. I was still alive but a part of me just died.

He found me. Alive. He broke open the shelf and aggressively tried to draw me closer. He made an attempt to kiss my forehead.

I took the knife out of the shelf and slit his throat from ear to ear. I was completely soaked in blood, and the wall sprayed with gore and marked with red splashes.

I failed...

~~~teeth in love~~~

She called me, not once but twice with an impatient voice, so uncharacteristic of her, "Why are you not reaching? Oh, no! Quickly dear." Now I am waiting in my car near her office. I am over the moon now as most of the time I call her and she comes. A hedonic feeling kicks me. I am humming an erotic song, drumming my fingers impatiently on the wheel. I don't understand it. What is about this woman who is technically in her late 30s but looks like a svelte 20-something, who keeps me on tenterhooks with her whims and fancies? Right now, for example, she has decided what we are doing is all wrong and that we should move on, each our separate ways. I bet she is secretly invoking the nuns from her severe missionary school childhood to help her give up the 'path of sin' or something like that. Because certainly, we have sinned. In copious quintiles.

Reshmi is my mistress and truth to be told, an exceedingly difficult one. When a man has the financial means to support a family and hoard a woman like Reshmi on the side, he should not have bothered with difficulties. But my luck seems to be acting upon that count. I have known Reshmi practically all my life. We were in college together, and it's only because of my infernal stupidity that we did not end up as man and wife.

Although Reshmi's take on it is that we would both have gotten fed up with each other and non-stop sex fairly quickly and ended up divorcing each other. According to her, our association is too singularly carnal in nature to ensure long-term commitment. Maybe, it is tough to tell. Espccially since in the months after Reshmi and I got 'introduced' to each other, after nearly two decades. I have not had the slightest inclination to let her go again.

This is more than what can be said about Pritha, my wife, whom I met at the ripe old age of 30, while doing Master's degree belatedly and, subsequently, married a few years later. Don't get me wrong. She is an excellent soul, I am sure. But there is only so much hypochondriasis a man take before getting bored to death of yet another detailed inventory of blood sugar level fluctuations (and insulin injections), spinal fluid degeneration (and palliative physiotherapy) and pain attack (no cure for this one).

I think this last one freaks me out the most. I am never sure, when one of these 'attacks' happens, whether to call an ambulance to the ER or give the overweight, blissfully homespun Pritha a real good shake.

Reshmi, on the other hand, does not get a panic attack. Ever! She is quite capable, of course, of giving other people panic attacks. But having one herself? Very definitely no! For all her recent ruminations about committing the deadly sin of sleeping with another woman's husband, she is a remarkably cool customer who effortlessly keeps me wrapped around her little finger.

As far as I am concerned, we could have carried on in perfect equanimity indefinitely - the three of us - with me playing reliable husband and father about the house to keep Pritha happy and stealing moments at Reshmi's small apartment where I usually spend at least one night every week and have a set of freshly laundered clothes stashed for an emergency.

I daresay I get this feeling sometimes that Pritha has smelled something akin to rat since the time Reshmi moved to the city a year ago and my entire grumpy demeanour underwent a sea change. If so, she chooses to look the other way when I show up at home, in the morning after a night at Reshmi's place, looking dishevelled and idiotically happy. Pritha is not the type of woman who would throw a fit and jeopardize her home and health over a minor indiscretion. She is much too fond of her secure little existence.

Reshmi, on the other hand, is constantly upsetting the apple cart. As she zips out of her office building, waving cheerily to one of her colleagues, something catches my throat. I can never get over how good that woman looks.

"Here, baby," I jump out of the car to hold the door open on the passenger side. She flashes me one of her conspiratorial grins and ducks in. I am back at the wheel in a jiffy, and we're off.

"Where to," I ask casually.

"Aren't you going to ask me why I asked you to pick me up from work?"

"I don't care. I'm getting to see you. That's enough!"

"Aw, come off it. We need to get serious."

Warning bells go off my head. It will again be the same debate on 'deadly sin' she, of late, enters in to, even on the bed. Often she becomes incredibly stubborn at the height of extreme sexual moment. Now I find the same stubbornness on her face. I, to take her off from seriousness, push my face on her smoothly shaved armpit, wide opened in her long cut sleeveless blouse. No reaction from her. She looks straight outside and says, "Pritha met me in my office and had long talks in a coffee bar yesterday."

"Really?" I try to sound indifferent, distant while struggling to regain my composure.

"Yeah, she had called me. Mentioned she had something important to discuss." An uneasy pause. And then Reshmi continues, "She wants a divorce, does not want to stand in the way between us."

"What?" my fake composure is in shreds now, and I am even bothering to pretend otherwise. "Why would she want to tell you that instead of me? She barely knows you."

"That's what made it easier for her to talk to me; she said she couldn't bring herself to confront you. She is a quiet type of person but determined for divorce since you have cheated her, and so she expects generous alimony, for, she'll have to raise Ron single-handedly."

Ron with her? Alimony? My foot. "I'll fight her in the court," I explode finally.

"But you can't. She'll bring the charge of adultery."

"Without a shred of proof?"

"I am the proof," she said it firmly.

"You? You? Are you in your senses?" I shouted.

"Don't shout. For the last one month, Pritha and I have met many times. She told me everything about you."

"What everything?" I am losing all my composures.

"She told me I am not the only woman, you have an extramarital affair with."

"That's damn lying. I swear to you, I have never been with anyone except you."

"That's not what Pritha gave me to understand."

"Listen, I used to feel guilty about wrecking your marriage until I realized you were ruining my whole life. Pritha was right. You are one unfeeling monster, and you would start treating me exactly as you treat her from day one of your marriage. I am glad she picked up the phone on that very day, though accidentally, instead of you."

"She misled you. Since you don't believe me, I promise, I will divorce her, give the demanded alimony. Then, Reshmi, we can get married and have a family…"

"Stop, you bastard! I never want to marry… Apparently, you were incapable of fathering a child, and Pritha knew you wanted one baby. She did you the favour of being unfaithful just once by sleeping with a genetically suitable partner. Ron, apparently, was the result of a lot of hard work. But not yours, Mr. Casanova."

I resist the urge to hit her "Get down," I say through my teeth. She does.

Four months later

Ron turns to smile, and I wave as I drop him off at school. My next stop is to the hospital where I need to pick up Pritha's blood report. Her blood sugar levels have been steady of late, but every few weeks she gets blood work done just to be on the safe side. Between her delicate state of health, the embarrassment accompanying lawsuits and need to provide a stable home for Ron, things managed to transpire such that words like 'divorce' or 'adultery' were not uttered again.

In any case, Reshmi left this town for good, after she had a nervous breakdown for the first time in her life. I expect, Pritha told her we are having another baby.

~~~the letter~~~

I woke up to a letter that day. A letter wasn't so usual in 2012; and, I had not received a personal one for ages. I stared at the square brown envelope for a while. It was mutely screeching for help from under the doorstep. I could make out from the lettering on the envelope that it was not one of those printed bank statements which regularly crowded my apartment door; rather, its lacklustre and dog-eared state made its pain in reaching me apparent. Someone had tried very hard to tell me something, and find me. It better be good. I picked it up and relieved it of its agony. Then I saw my name, and several of my addresses, re-directed to several other of mine, written on it in many handwritings. The handwriting, which had begun this letter, did not seem familiar.

Coffee in hand, my groggy-but-not-so-sleepy-eyes began to read the dirty blue pages of the decrepit letter:

I don't know where you live now. But I have to share this moment's story with you. Do you remember the beach, its waves, and the towering black clouds running after us? But you also remember that we weren't running. Today I know why. Perhaps, you would think that several of the bugs in my head have started stirring, but I assure you, I have never felt more confident in my life about what I am going to do. I don't even know whether you remember me.

For me, it was arduous to forget you. It is because you happened for that time and then vanished: a memory difficult to ignore. It's like a dream which one clings on to because it is something fantastic, though it wouldn't really qualify as a promise for the future or a cushion for the past. That day did not demand that I remember it, so I have remembered it countless times, day after day, night after night, like an obsession in playing a song over and over again every day for a good long fifteen-day vacation.

I must come to the point. You had asked me that day, under the thatch, why I wouldn't make love to you. I wasn't ready with a suitable answer. I think I now know. I wouldn't have remembered you if I had made love to you, my dear. That's the truth. It is not vaguely in the romantic vein that I say this, rather the opposite, I know. Who would dare to underestimate the opulence of making love on the white sands of the pristine beach on a cloudy afternoon, and most importantly, why? Again, I need to digress. I need to tell you that it was not that I did not feel like making love to you. I had painfully resisted myself to savour every bit of you. I touched you many times, and I kissed you. And we shared bits of our lives. The beer was enriching every pore of my body, heating me up from within. I was beginning to get so fond of you that alcohol didn't seem to mind giving me all the naughty ideas. I didn't know then that that day or its resonating imageries would make me spend many an afternoon from doing anything else, concrete or otherwise.

I know I had let you down when I held your hand and insisted we go for a walk instead. But then you apprehended a storm, my love. And then you shouted, 'Oh, it is so exquisite!' A strange thing to say ahead of a storm, *mon amie*, but so refreshing! You exclaimed as the murky clouds overwhelmed the sky, with the wind finally trailing us, as we were girdled in frantic bursts of squalls. The wind was just a zephyr at first; then the granules of sand pricked our legs. Your bare legs encountered the sandy delirium; you cried out, 'Shut your eyes! The sand will get in!' You covered my eyes with your hands, as you shut yours tightly. As the gale intensified, and the sea swayed in a tumultuous riot, we stood, feeling the salt, water and wind. That brought me happiness. And that trice made me live the ocean, its blue depths and its frothy bosoms and whispered love so many times bigger than you or me.

But, underneath all this, lies one deception. You had no need to know this, but I can't live with these compliant custodians of recollections happily, and not tell you of the one thing I should have said to you that day. I saw life through you, my girl: I am blind and was always so. Let me not spell it out and spoil it for you.

The day we shared was incomplete in more than one way, but it has completed me for this life and many more. I do not know how you look, but I know you are not afraid of an approaching storm. And I have looked within you as many times as I have looked within my own havens... without my eyes... and I have seen the seagulls fly across the vista.

From
The liar on the beach

Forgetting gnaws on one's past till emaciated hollow events are uprooted from one's life. Still, fading fleeting moments are difficult to savour: one doesn't know how to accrue all the conjectural nonfigurative moods that give birth to a stream of other such thoughts, in attempting to savour the heart of such moments. I closed my eyes. Suddenly in one moment, a day twelve years ago in my life, and all the mirth and confusions it had brought with it sprang to life. It is difficult to remember the feeling one gets when swept over by beauty, it is traumatizing to watch the memory of the feeling leave one as fast it had come. But that morning, it all came back - not with a jolt, but slowly swathing me and drowning me in timelessness. Not just the day, but the day with its every vein and artery. Letters can make the world go round. This one made me sail.

~~~riju~~~

That particular day, it was drizzling since morning. Dark grey clouds cast a shadow of boredom and restlessness over the city. Phalgu sat lost in thought by the window of his room, overseeing the wet garden. He wished the rain would stop, and Riju would come to play with him. But, the day continued to be droopy and inattentive to the child's temptations. He sucked the ice cream his grandmother made for him and kept wishing Riju would turn up.

In the afternoon, the rain stopped; it wasn't ideal weather to play out in the open. However, when Riju came running up the stairs, Phalgu jumped for joy. "Let's go to the terrace," Riju chimed. "It is locked," Phalgu said, feeling sorry to let his friend down.

Phalgu's house had a huge terrace, with walls which ran like mazes all over the area, making it an ideal place for hide-and-seek, and other such games.

"Where is the key?" Riju was indeed adamant.

"It is under Dida's pillow," Phalgu apprehensively said, knowing full well what he would be expected to do then.

As they approached his grandmother's room, they could see her sitting by the window, legs stretched, cutting her supari into little pieces with a jnati.

Phalgu was always afraid of the instrument; he had once hurt his little finger by it. Since then, he had been petrified of the jnati and was not very fond of its twisted shape. Phalgu always liked symmetrical things, the jnati had intrigued him because he had seen his sister playing with it one day, and she had put on a red cloth on it to make it appear like a woman in a *ghomta*. But ever since his finger blew up like a balloon, and throbbed and pained, he dismissed it as an ugly thing.

As they peeped inside the room, Riju urged him to go inside. Phalgu was sure his grandmother would notice the slightest movement. Her bed was old-fashioned, and had quite a height; it could easily cover Phalgu if he slipped by it, but, how would he enter without being noticed? So, as Phalgu stood there not knowing what to do, he looked at Riju. No one was beside him! Where did he go? Phalgu leaned back, careful not to make any sound, and looked left and right. He couldn't see Riju anywhere. He was right here, where did he vanish in so little time? He turned to look at the room once again. Suddenly, near his leg, he could see Riju slithering away like a snake under the bed. As Phalgu watched the brilliant act of acrobatics, Riju slipped under the bed, sat up, and quietly lifted his left hand and shoved it under the pillow. Few moments of a frantic search and the smile on his face confirmed victory. As the stealth concluded, he slipped out of the room in ease, and soon, both were on their way up the stairs.

As Riju unlocked the door of the terrace, Phalgu congratulated him. "You are good. But be careful, Dida notices all the little things," he said. "No, I am sure she didn't notice this time. She won't look for the key anytime soon, no?" Riju asked. "Uhhh…no, I don't think so. She will not look for it today, as there are no washed clothes drying out there. Thanks to the rain, at least it did us some good," Phalgu said and grinned.

The terrace was too risky to be run about on. It was slippery, and the moss wouldn't spare their limbs. Hence, Riju decided it was best to play Pirates.

"Cutlass," Riju said, and both drew out their imaginary swords from their waist and swung them.

"Ahoy, me Hearties!" they said aloud. Soon, Riju was walking on the parapet which hung out of the terrace wall. Risky and precarious were what interested them. As Riju paced up and down the parapet, Phalgu shouted, "Yo, ho, ho, and a bottle of rum." The slimy moss on the parapet grinned maliciously.

As Phalgu's grandmother strolled into the kitchen, which was on the second storey, she adjusted her sari *anchol* and swished it backwards on her left shoulders. She held her knees in pain, after climbing the steep flight of stairs. While reaching out on the shelves, she grumbled, as her stiff joints groaned with pain. This often prohibited her from many a daily activity she was used to.

As she stood rubbing her arm, her face twisted with pain, she looked out of the window. And what did she see? Two little legs dangling and frantically wanting to get back to where they were! "Phaaaalguuuuu," the shrill voice reached every nook and corner of the house, and it sure did not go unnoticed by the pirates.

While Riju dangled in mid-air, Phalgu was of no help. He couldn't drag him up again; it was impossible to reach out to the dangling figure, let alone pull him up. Riju kept hanging from the parapet.

"Get up," Phalgu shouted. "She knows we are here," he was sweating profusely. Riju suddenly heaved himself up with a huge force back to the parapet. Soon, they were unlocking the door and climbing downstairs. His grandmother was walking towards the terrace, but it would take her considerable time to walk past many corridors, and this was the time they had to use best. They ran downstairs and sneaked into the little hut, where Diwakar kaka stayed, and who was gardening, as usual, plucking the weeds and washing the dirt which had accumulated, after the constant drizzle. As Phalgu and Riju waited there, Phalgu's mother walked in from the main gate. She was back from school. This sent ripples of trepidation in the little Bravehearts. They were done for!

As his mother entered the house, Phalgu implored Riju to run away.

"Go, go, go. Wait, you have cut yourself there," he said as he looked at Riju's knee. There was a huge uncouth cut on his knee; it must have rubbed on the wall while he had somersaulted back on the parapet.

"That's alright. Are you sure you want to face your mother alone?" Riju asked.

"Of course. You run. Don't worry about me. I will handle it," Phalgu said as Riju made a run for his life.

Phalgu quietly tip-toed into the house, walked straight down the long corridor, turned right, and walked into his grandmother's room. It was obviously empty. He could hear his grandmother from the second storey complain to his mother about how naughty Phalgu was, and that he had gone to the terrace and what a shock she got when she saw… it went on and on and on. Phalgu shut his ears with his hands; he did not want to hear any more of this. He put the key back under his grandmother's pillow, and ran into his own room, and threw himself on the bed. First, he thought he would feign sleep; then he changed his mind. He took out a Professor Shanku novel from his shelf and started reading it, lying on his belly. He would simply deny having gone to the terrace when his mother asked.

It had hardly been five minutes when his mother stormed inside his room with a long stick in her hand; God knows where she got these sticks from whenever she needed them.

Phalgu had once tried to look for the place where she hid them, but it was of no help.

"Did you go to the terrace?" she asked. He could tell that she was furious; her eyebrows looked like one long furry worm; her nostrils were inflated, her cheeks were red, and her lips were tightly drawn together.

"No, when? What are you talking about?" Phalgu stared at her as if she had said something improbable, while he really hoped his innocent face did the trick.

"Get up!" she screamed and threw his book on the floor. Phalgu sadly looked at the book and slowly sat up on the bed.

"What is this?" she screamed as she pointed to Phalgu's knee. The huge cut was dripping blood, a thin trail of which was slowly running down his leg. To make matters worse, Phalgu's father returned home early that evening amid the commotion. Just as he was rubbing his dirty feet on the mat outside the door, the infuriated woman rushed to him, the stick still in her hand, and said, "Look what he has done again! He slipped from the parapet. He stole the keys from Ma's room..." His eyes red with fury, his lips quaking, Phalgu's father's growl had made the walls tremble that day,

"Riju, come here. Now!"

~~~the answer~~~

Yellow light in a stream from above in an otherwise dark hall; a drone of murmur from all around, from similarly yellow-lit tables; and two among many, looking for stealing a moment to themselves. She wasn't listening to anything any of them were saying. She wished she could elegantly earn solitude, not having to explain much. Explaining complicated ideas was never her favourite. However, people were always intrigued by loners, as if the meaning of life lay in unravelling the complicated rigmaroles, which like any other, loners boast of possessing.

Why they choose loners is hidden in the fact that silence is often naively connected to secrecy and secrecy to sin. One must be an open book, one must be transparent, and one must always be truthful. What if I am an open book, and you turn the first page, your face twists; your lips quiver, your eyes are bloodshot, as you turn the yellows one by one at first and then in a frenzy; and by the time you have reached the jaundiced fag-end, you want to scream, puke and throttle me? What if I am transparent, and let you see through me, choosing the glitzy alleys of me, guiding you through the whites, a little bit of grey perhaps to keep in touch with reality, would you dig out and explore the dark crooks from the depths of my bosom? Would you really see through me? Oh, and must I never lie?…

The silhouette rises, gently as a fading shadow, and then grows brighter, and then stops. Her breath stops. A hand hangs mid-air in invitation, and a voice rings: Shall we? A waltz fills the place, and she rises like his shadow, like a feather. They stand in the ring locked in each other, and then she feels warm around the waist, and they move like two leaves in the wind. She closes her eyes, and lets the music rip her apart; she feels the breeze and feels afloat, barely being able to feel her limbs; and then she dreams.

"It's a waltz, you know. Do you close your eyes every time?" Her eyes open, she looks at him, she finds him looking at her and tries to focus.

"No, I don't. But this... this is Gertrude's Dream Waltz. I am sorry, did I trip?"

"No. I like this symphony too."

She didn't know he liked Beethoven. Never quite found out. She asks, "Do you like all of Beethoven? Because this is not really him, you know. This is not like the rest he has done."

"Hm, yeah... some don't think he composed it."

"What do you think?"

"I am thankful it is there, Beethoven or not..."

She lifts her chin and directs her gaze sideways, a high-chinned duchess untouched. She breathes heavily while she kills the urge to look into the burning flame.

He turns her about, touching her at the crucial and significant turns, he guides her through gorges and crevices, he glides her over canyons and rivulets unscathed. She lets him take her every time, blindly determined to follow - certain paradoxes mean more than life, and they are like corrosive acid, silently burning irreplaceable holes through you. But... must one always chase the illusion it drives one to?

Then with a gentle swish, he is by her side, leading her on; he clasps her left hand in his and places them on his chest. She fights back her tears. But they must spill once the chasm can't hold them anymore. She doesn't have to try hard to remember all that she shouldn't. She remembers their walk on the autumn leaves; she remembers the night when they had met; and she remembers the swim they took in the restless frothy water, skin against skin, blood against blood. Whoosh, and she is face to face with him again... but is she really?

The moonlight is a beauty; she tip-toes to the dance floor and floods them in blue light. Oh, must she be so cruel? She sees his forehead, lines etched deep. She looks away; she can't look at him, not just yet. She wants to plunge in his arms and sob, she wants to touch him deep within.

She can't hold back her tears any longer, she must let them go. She looks at him, the first time through the dance, and the water comes trickling down, her tears find their way. The music dies. They stop, they bow. He holds her hand and leads her away from the dance floor. He walks by her side, at a slow pace, and talks to her.

"Thank you, you are remarkable." She manages to say thank you. He looks at her and asks,

"Will you remember this night?"

She stops walking. She turns to him. No word in any language would agree to deceive her at this moment. She simply cannot speak. She feels wretched and broken. She thinks of everything together, and she feels light-headed. But she cannot take her eyes off him...

From a distance, a man approaches and takes her by her arm, and whispers, "It is getting late, shouldn't we be back by now? We have an early flight." He flashes a smile at him too.

A last glance, and he looks tired and washed. Before turning back and walking away, he smiles and says, "But, you owe me the answer."

For, how long does music play, for how long does it last?

~~~blind luck~~~

Running like a half-wit person, sweating under the fierce glare of the afternoon sun, I looked left and then right and finally came to a halt. My breathing could be heard so loud that it could put a stethoscope to shame. Delirious because of the afternoon heat, I decided to give up the search. As soon as I turned to head back to the bookstore, I collided and fell flat on the ground. Unable to feel my hands, I thought I had died. A gentle spray of water helped me regain my consciousness.

"Are you alright?" asked a male voice.

"I guess," I stammered.

Squinting my eyes to recognize the face of the person standing before me, I tried to get up. Aching limbs and bruised palms didn't quite let me up though. He helped me get up and then asked, "Do I dazzle you?"

"What?" I asked.

"You didn't understand, did you?"

"No, I didn't," I said, agitated at the irrelevant conversation that was taking away my energy.

He didn't explain any further. It did not take rocket science for me to connect the dots and understand what he was trying to say. He was the same man whom I was chasing or rather searching for. He was the one with whom I had participated in the 'Bookoholics - Carry on the Conversation' competition. He was too good at it. And I had made a run for him after the event was over because I wanted to return his copy of 'Postscript'.

A few hours before

Bored and jobless on a weekday, I decided to go to Crossword and check out the new books. I had taken a day off as my client, too, was on leave, and I didn't have much to do without him. What better occasion than this to take a day off! As I packed a few essentials into my sling bag, my dog, Silver, jumped on me and pushed me hard on the sofa. Silver ruined my yellow dress and made me change into a pastel blue coloured t-shirt. Why these details are essential, you might ask? Well, it was this blue t-shirt that made me get selected for the competition.

That's the thing about Crossword. They are so dynamic. They keep on organizing such promotional events, and the reviewers and the bloggers can get the best out of such competitions. 'Bookaholics - Carry on the Conversation' was one such competition. Each participant was randomly paired with another, and they had to prove their knowledge of the books by first identifying the speaker (character) and then completing the dialogue. The selectors just announced "All blues pair together" and there it went. With no blue shirt in sight, I felt dejected. But just then someone spoke, "This is the door to both sustenance and sanity. And we are each other's key."

I couldn't help but pass a smile. He was a Hunger Games fan, and I knew it that very instant that our pair would easily win this competition.

"Hi, I am Purab. I don't think anyone else is in blue so you will have to bear with me while I poke my brain cells to win this game." He finished in one breath.

"Hi, I am Preeshi. I don't mind bearing the brunt of your actions as long as the brunt is sweet!" I tried to sound smarter.

"Our names alliterate! Such a positive coincidence," he concluded. He offered me to take his hand and we headed to the main stage where the book nerds had already huddled up.

After a series of dialogues to complete, we waited with bated breath for the last set. The moderator handed Purab a chit. Already a bundle of nerves, I stared at him, waiting for him to deliver his line. I only had 10 seconds to identify the character whose line he would be delivering and another 20 seconds to complete the conversation.

"My family, we're different from others of our kind. We only hunt animals. We've learned to control our thirst but it's you, your scent, it's like a drug to me. You're like you're my own personal brand of heroin," said Purab and waited.

My mind was in jitters. I knew this line so well that I had forgotten the source! Purab had started getting heebie-jeebies by then.

"Why did you hate me so much when we met?" I asked.

"I did, only because of wanting you so badly. I still don't know if I can control myself," he muttered.

"I know you can," I comforted.

"Yes, we know you both can, and you have done it. Congratulations on winning this competition" shouted the moderator.

Overwhelmed with joy, Purab and I hugged each other but the invisible societal bounds made us realize the repercussions of our actions quickly. We chatted for a little while before parting ways. I got to know that he was an avid reader and worked in an IT company.

Fast forward a few hours, and there we were on the street, facing each other again.

"What is my book doing in your bag?" He questioned.

"You had dropped it in the store. So I was running behind you to return it."

"Did you open it or read it?"

"Why would I do that? Do you doubt me?" I rebuked.

"Preeshi, how can you not open a book when you find it!"

I didn't understand what he meant. It was only when my roommate suggested that he might have left his phone number in the book that I had my light bulb moment. But it was too late, wasn't it?

Days passed in a jiffy and I couldn't even spend one moment not thinking about him. His dishevelled teased platinum hair, ramrod straight and rock-jawed, with gunmetal eyes and shoulders that seemed mitred at a perfect ninety-degree angle- all of these kept flashing before my eyes. Was I in love? I couldn't possibly be as I had only met him once. That was impractical. I tried to brush aside these thoughts before they took over my thinking ability.

"Preeshi, come down for breakfast," shouted Amita, my roommate.

"Coming in five," I shouted back.

"There is someone to meet you. Scurry downstairs, now!" Amita chided.

Who would have come to meet me on a Sunday, I wondered. As I paced down the stairs, I realized that I looked as ugly as a duckling. With my hair all over the face, my kohl spread like butter on my cheeks and my tousled head, I was sure to scare away the visitor.

"You? What are you doing here? How did you know that I lived here?" I shot an array of questions.

Purab's mystified look made me curse my folly. While on one hand, I wished to see him so desperately, I didn't even think twice before shooting so many questions at him.

"Calm down, Preeshi. I just read the book that you left for me on the road."

"Book? Which book? When did I leave any book?" I tried pretending.

"Really? You might not be eager to read the notes left behind in someone else's book, but I am. I found your address in 'Every Breath' that you left on the road. You had bookmarked the page with the bill! Who does that?" He shot a disgusted look.

"I do that. What's wrong in that? At least you got to know my address, didn't you?"

"Yes, I did. Now make my effort worthwhile by agreeing to come for a coffee with me," he grinned.

Smiling faintly, I gestured to Amita that I would be having breakfast outside. Rushing upstairs to do a slight touch up, I asked Purab to sit and read for a while. What followed next was a series of outings where two Literature enthusiasts shared optimism, memorable dialogues and delved deeper into the world of love where twilight brought hope, letters brought back memories and bottles carried messages of love.

~~~cafuné~~~

A gentle breeze wafts in, the sea playfully creeps into the beach and the early morning sun rays dance on the waves. The beach is almost empty, apart from the young man seemingly lost in the way the water and light twinkle. The play of light and water reminds him of her twinkling eyes and laughter.

He remembers her laughter – as effervescent and as unaffected as these playful waves. Tears and sea breeze sting his eyes. Dev doesn't stop the tears today. He allows them to flow out and mix in with the vast ocean. Her note is still in his fist. He opens it, reads it. And lets it drop in the waves with the hope that the sea will take it all away.

But they say the sea never keeps anything. It returns what it takes.

"Will it return my heart; will it return her to me?" for a moment Dev thinks wishfully.

"No. It can't," he knows… her letter had said, "We of those times, no longer the same."

He had rushed to Goa, thinking that this is the best place to go to when you wish to heal a grieving heart. He felt rather than brooding about the past, it's best to focus on his book on Indian flowers.

A perfumer, Tania Roderick from Goa, who is unveiling her new fragrance, had invited him for the launch. Dev had instantly taken up her request and agreed to be a part of that walk and interact with the press. This would be a good distraction he had thought.

Dev had been staring at the sea for what seemed like an eternity. Snapping out of his thoughts, he realizes there's someone else on the beach. She is a vision. Dressed in a white kaftan coverup over an emerald green bikini and with her sun-kissed, cascading hair, she looks ethereal. She smiles at him. He stops staring and smiles back.

"Hi, I am Dev Roy," he introduces himself.

"I am Kady… Kadambari," she says.

He observes her glistening, deep brown eyes twinkle. There are green specs that make them look like the sea. A delicate, frangipani flower is tucked behind her ear.

He asks her if she is here for the perfume launch. She nods.

She sits down on the beach and starts scrubbing her hands and feet with sand and water. Dev sits down next to her. They sit together in silence for a while.

He closes his eyes and lies down, aware that she is watching him, but it doesn't feel like an intrusion. He cries. She sits next to him and hears him sob. Sometimes you just need someone to hear you cry your heart out.

Dev walks back to his room from the beach while taking a quick round of the resort – Frangipani. It's a quaint place, a cluster of small Goan cottages with a frangipani tree in front of each villa.

As he walks his hand gently grazes over the lemongrass hedge, letting out their strong citrusy aroma with his touch.

Around 7:30 PM Dev returns to the beach, that's the venue for tonight. It's a balmy evening. The air is humid though. His cotton shirt clings to his tall, lean form… sticking to his skin, the way it used to when she would weep on his shoulders, and he would be soaked in her tears and his sweat.

He blinks away his tears as he approaches Tania, and she hands him a small bottle of her perfume. It's an intriguing scent that she has created – a subtle medley of lavender, frangipani, lemongrass and bergamot essential oils. The fragrance is poetically named Cafuné, which Tania explains to him is a Portuguese word meaning the act of tenderly running fingers through one's lover's hair.

Late into the night, Dev lazes around on the deck chairs with the journalists. He looks for her, but he can't see Kadambari anywhere.

There is something about the night tonight, the intoxication of the coconut feni, sound of the waves, the salty smell of the sea, the sharpness of the ocean breeze, the lovely sight of the sky kissing the sea and bitter-sour flavour of the drink.

His heart feels a little lighter. He opens the playlist on his phone and taps on Nusrat Fateh Ali Khan's Qawwalis. Dev feels a touch. Like someone caressing his hair.

He opens his eyes and sees Kadambari, lounging on the deck chair next to him. "Raag Malkauns," says she. She is now wearing an inky blue kaftan dress and has a frangipani bloom tucked behind her ear.

"This is Khan Saab's rendition of Raag Malkauns," she explains further. "It's a night Raag and resonates with spirits like us."

"Impressive," says Dev and plays for her, "*Tum Ek Gorakh Dhanda Ho...*"

"Which Raag is this?" he asks her.

She listens to it carefully, asking him to replay a few portions.

Ho bhi nahi aur har ja ho,
Ho bhi nahi aur har ja ho
Tum ek gorakh dhanda ho

"Could be Raag Kalyan, not sure... could also be Raag Darbari," she says with a smile.

As they walk on the beach, the waves caress their feet; their hands brush against each other, sometimes their fingers interlock, and at times they don't. Time stands still, or have they lost track of time. From Nusrat, they have moved to Farida Khanum's *'Aaj Jaane Ki Zid Na Karo'*.

"This is Raag Khayam," she says, gently looking up to Dev. They have reached back to the resort rooms.

But neither of them wants to leave, just yet. They embrace and slowly kiss under the frangipani tree. It starts to drizzle, and they walk back in the rain to the mystical sea.

At about 2 AM Dev finally returns to his room. All he manages to do is kick off his loafers, slip into his bed and drift into a deep, deep sleep.

He wakes up with a soft but consistent knock at the door. The AC is off. He feels groggy and dizzy. The feni was strong. His head aches, and the knocking at the door continues.

'Could it be Kadambari?' he thinks.

He pulls himself out of bed, opens the door, and a gentle breeze blows in. It's pitch dark outside and not a soul in sight.

'I must have been dreaming,' he assumes and closes the door and goes back to bed. The knocking starts again, he ignores it, but the room feels stuffy without the AC. He finally decides to call the housekeeping. It is 3:20 in the morning.

The staff arrives within a few minutes. The AC had tripped, they say. It's fixed now, and the room starts getting cooler. The knocking, they tell him, must have been the wind or some night bird. The housekeeping team leaves, and he tumbles back into the bed. But that damn knocking starts again. He pulls a pillow over his head and tries to sleep.

He has visions of Kadambari. Dev tosses and turns and finally decides to get out of bed at 5 AM. He goes for a run on the beach.

After a shower, he goes for breakfast. He looks for Kadambari but can't find her anywhere. Perhaps she is sleeping in late.

It's a hot afternoon. Dev, Tania and the journalists are in Mapusa town. It's a busy Friday. From shortest of denim shorts to antique doorknobs, dried fish, spices, flowers and perfume oils, the small make-shift stalls have a medley of wares to sell. Dev buys some spices and fresh flowers.

Then he sees Kadambari. The delicate frangipani flower that she had been tucked behind her ear yesterday has now been replaced by a robust desi Gulab. She is wearing a bright yellow sundress with a marigold garland around her neck and a string of jasmine around her wrist.

Dev goes over to the stall where Kadambari is waiting for him. She tells him that this is her favourite shop. With her help, he picks up some interesting incense sticks – lotus, patchouli, sage, lemongrass.

The shopkeeper is an ancient woman with deep, penetrating eyes. As she looks into Dev's eyes, he feels as if she is looking into his soul. She tells him, "Please light the patchouli incense stick in your room today. It will protect you."

'Protect me? From what?' Dev wonders.

By the time Dev returns from Mapusa, it's early evening. As the sun sets, he lights the patchouli incense, wears a blue and white Hawaiian-style shirt over his denim shorts, picks up a frangipani flower from the ground beneath the tree and heads to the venue.

Fire breathers, live music, Mehendi artists, tattoo artists, it's like a mini carnival. And amidst all this, the perfume is ceremoniously 'launched'.

The faint scent of the flower fills the night air. Dev makes his way to the bar, where he sees Kadambari in a white crochet dress with her hair tied up with a red ribbon.

Their glasses of white wine Sangria arrive. They clink their glasses, take a sip and instinctively start walking towards the beach. They walk in silence for a long time, and then the thunder and rain roll in. Soaked to their skin, they kiss in the rain and make their way back to the frangipani tree next to his room. They kiss under the tree again.

She leads him to his room, holding his hand. They draw out the curtains and sit on the floor, watching the rain melt on the window. Kadambari scatters a handful of frangipani flowers on the floor.

At 3 AM, the knocking starts again. Dev's head is pounding. Kadambari is not there, she must have gone back to her room. The knocking continues, and he just lets it be.

He wakes up at 5 in the morning. He has had strange dreams - the sea, Kadambari walking into the sea, a frangipani tree. He drifts off into a slumber.

Dev wakes up looking at the ceiling. Are those impressions of footmarks on it? He thinks it was there before. Or was it? Maybe he had not noticed it. He wondered how the footprints could have been formed on the ceiling. Perhaps, someone had walked on the terrace above when the cottage was being built. That's the best explanation that he can think of. He gets out of his bed to get ready.

He has a frail frangipani flower in his fist. Where did that come from? It must be one of the flowers that Kadambari had scattered on the floor.

He is running a little late. He has a meeting with Tania scheduled. He looks at the wall clock; it is almost 10 AM. 'I need to hurry', he thinks, and then he notices something even stranger.

There are foot impressions all over the wall. Starting from the ground level up to the ceiling, as if someone had walked up the wall. Perhaps it is wallpaper. A wallpaper with foot impressions. What else can it be?

Dev pushes the thought out of his mind and starts getting ready to leave. He also has to meet Kadambari, and he doesn't even have her number.

He is distracted while speaking to Tania. She observes that and asks him how he is.

Dev tells her about the knocking on the door, the AC tripping, the foot impressions on the wall and Kadambari.

"Who…Who is Kadambari?" Tania asks.

He tells her he is referring to Kadambari, the journalist who is staying in the room diagonally opposite his.

"Dev, there's no journalist here by the name Kadambari," says Tania. "And the room that you are talking about is cottage 9 that's under repair."

"Oh, okay then she must be some other guest in another room," he tells Tania while getting up to leave.

"Dev, there's no other guest in the resort apart from our group, we have booked the entire hotel," Tania says with a serious and concerned look.

Dev leaves for the airport with these lyrics playing in a loop in his head.

Ho bhi nahi aur har ja ho,
Ho bhi nahi aur har ja ho
Tum ek gorakh dhanda ho

Kadambari smiles.

~~~petrichor~~~

Parijaat wakes up dreaming of smell - a fragrance that she knows, but can't pinpoint where she could have smelt it before. She opens one eye to look at the watch, it's almost 5 AM. She has a flight to catch in a couple of hours. Parijaat wonders if she could afford to sleep just a little more... The AC is humming gently... the room temperature is just right... the Jaipuri *rajai* is... hmm... so comfortable.

It's raining... Small rivulets are running down the cool window pane of her room. Parijaat finds it fascinating to part the curtain a little, touch the cool glass pane with her soft, slender fingers and trace the water droplets gently hitting gliding down the glass.

A couple of months ago, Parijaat had taken a hypnotherapy session during which she had recalled a pleasant memory of going back to her ancestral home in Kurseong and then suddenly in that trance, she saw a pair of bright brown sparkling eyes. The eyes of someone who she has known for very... very long, someone who meant a lot to her... but who was it? And why did it tug at her heartstrings to see these eyes? She couldn't explain.

Parijaat hadn't been to Kurseong for more than a decade now. It was before her ancestral home was sold off and turned into a boutique hotel. With each passing day, her longing for the sleepy town and her old home had grown deeper and deeper. Finally, she decided that she would have to go there to figure out what was calling her to those hills.

So here she is now at the Bagdogra Airport getting into the taxi that the guest house has sent to drive her up to Kurseong. As she settles into the cab, she is told by Suraj, the cab driver, that there's another guest, a co-passenger.

She sees a tall man of athletic built, maybe in his 30s walk towards the car. He is wearing moss green reflectors and an Arsenal jacket over his faded jeans.

"So sorry to keep you waiting," her co-passenger apologises to Parijaat and introduces himself as Rudra Choudhury.

"I am Parijaat Sen," Parijaat replies.

The cab starts moving out of the airport. After the hustle-bustle of Bagdogra market, the car slowly makes its way through the Sukna Forest. There's a distinct change in the air, as the roads loop upwards the temperature drops at every turn, the sound of dry leaves getting crushed under the wheels... Parijaat's ears get blocked, and her face is gently caressed by the cool, moist fog - balm for the soul.

She feels this damp, fresh air bathe the insides of her throat, lungs, heart, arteries, capillaries, it fills in her being as she drifts into slumber.

Someone gently nudges her awake, softly whispering, "Don't fall asleep in the car sweetheart."

"Who said that?" Parijaat wonders - Rudra is sleeping, Suraj is speaking to someone on the phone, then who? Must have been a dream, she assumes.

Soon they arrive at the Kurseong Tourist Lodge, which is just about a couple of kilometres from the hotel. As Parijaat lifts the lid of the bamboo basket, the steam from the momos touches her face and the smell of the chicken broth slowly warms its way into her heart.

"Ms Sen..." Rudra says.

"You can call me Parijaat," she replies.

Rudra is still wearing his reflectors, and Parijaat feels a little uncomfortable looking at her reflection on his eyewear. She feels a strong desire to see his eyes.

"You are here on vacation?" Rudra asks her, breaking her thoughts.

"Errr... No, for some... some work," Parijaat stammers, slightly embarrassed for staring at his eyes. She explains, "I am a writer... I am here in search of inspiration for my next book."

"That's very interesting and fancy... I mean fascinating," Rudra says with a laugh.

"What do you do?" Parijaat asks.

"I am a tea taster by profession and a perfumer by passion... here to visit some tea garden, while sniffing around for inspiration for my next perfume," he explains.

"That's pretty fancy yourself," Parijaat laughs.

And suddenly! A whistle blows... Parijaat feels a lurch in her heart, the drowsy chugging becomes clearer. The blue-black engine laboriously works itself up the winding tracks and gently lets off steam.

Parijaat looks at Rudra and reading her racing thoughts, he says, "Let's go!" Instinctively they grab each others' hands and make a dash to the cab.

Parijaat requests Suraj to follow the train for the last leg of their journey... the journey to St Mary's Hill, Ivy Cott.

As Parijaat stands on the stairs leading down to Ivy Cott, she runs her palm gently along the moss-covered wall, the velvety touch.

"This is my ancestral home," Parijaat shares with Rudra as they walk towards the reception.

That ancient smell wafts in as they enter the hotel. Parijaat inhales it and says, "Umm a mix of cedar and pine… fresh, clean, moist and woody… the scent of wet earth… this smell has a name."

"Petrichor," replies Rudra, "That's the word for it. It's the pleasant smell that accompanies the first rain after a spell of warm weather. That's the smell that I have been trying to create for a very long time."

"These hills always have this smell," Parijaat replies with a smile. She wishes that Rudra would take off his reflectors now.

As Parijaat freshens up in her room, she realises she hasn't really been this happy in a very long while. She takes her time to get ready for the evening. Her freshly washed hair gleams and shines. She slips on a moss green turtleneck over black silk tights and throws on a bright red shawl. She wears a scarlet lipstick, lines her large eyes with kohl, spritzes on a jasmine body mist and then heads towards the dining room.

The room is almost empty, only Rudra is sitting at a table by the window with a host of tea cups lined up before him. He looks up and waves at her to join him at his table. Parijaat walks over to him and sits down.

"Tea tasting?" Parijaat asks him.

"Why don't you try it too?" says Rudra. "First inhale the aroma, take a sip of the brew, swirl it and swish it in your mouth and then gulp it down."

Rudra offers Parijaat a small portion of the tea liquor, "It's a white tea," he explains.

Parijaat takes a sip and tries to swish it in her mouth and gently drink it.

"Tea maybe a gentle drink but to taste it you need to let go of inhibitions," Rudra tells her, "Slurp it up and swish it the way you would gargle... let all the flavours open up in your mouth."

Parijaat tries it again... this time with a little more confidence... as they move from one tea to another, the shell that she had built around her gets chipped, little at a time. Slowly the room fills in with other guests and a karaoke evening begins.

By then, Parijaat is high on tea and nostalgia. She remembers how she and her cousins would sing and dance in this very room.

"Why don't you sing?" Rudra gently encourages her. With the microphone in her hand, there's no holding back. With playful abandon, Parijaat breaks into her favourite song... *Hawa Hawai.*

Cedarwood, pine, earth, moss, fresh grass, rain... Parijaat wakes up smelling that scent... it's 5 AM now. She recalls she is in Ivy Cott. There's a black jay or a magpie cawing somewhere in the hills.

Parijaat's phone buzzes. It's a message from Rudra.

"Hello, *Hawa Hawai*! What a rockstar you are, wake up. You spoke about the grotto last night. I am here. Would you like to join me?" read his text.

"Sure," texts back Parijaat.

When she reaches the grotto, she finds Rudra engrossed in exploring the cave... smelling the grass, the bark of the trees, crushed leaves. Parijaat lies down on the grass, under that ancient pine tree, the way she would always as a child. She closes her eyes and tries to remember the summers that she had spent here. Rudra lies down next to her, their hands brush against each other and his fresh, clean scent envelops her. A smell of comfort, the smell of Kurseong, almost.

"Are you afraid of ghosts?" Rudra asks her.

"No, I am not. I have made friends with them," trails off Parijaat. Rudra's fingers entwine with hers, but his voice starts fading away as her mind wanders off... Rustling leaves... smell of smokey tobacco.

She is walking through the woods near the grotto. A gentle breeze, smell of cedar. She loves this rough surface of the pine tree. She strains her eyes to catch the top of the tree. A hummingbird somewhere? She's not sure if it's a hummingbird.

"It is a hummingbird," says a deep voice near her. She turns around and faces a man. She can't decide if he is young or old... odd... he could be 28 or 68 or even 88. He wears thick glasses that almost blur out his eyes but he looks familiar, like who?

"It's a hummingbird," he repeats and smiles. His name is Shiv, he tells her. He is a photographer and shows Parijaat his camera. It looks vintage, just like himself. It's a Hasselblad from the 1920s, he explains.

He is an intriguing man, and as they walk, that smell of the forest gets stronger.

"May I click a picture of yours," Shiv asks her, "You will have it by tonight," he promises. Parijaat stops under a cedar tree and Shiv clicks a picture of her.

As they walk and talk, Parijaat realises that Shiv knew her grandparents pretty well. She has never seen her grandparents. Shiv tells Parijaat that her grandfather had passed away in Kurseong. That same month in March, her grandmother had returned to Kolkata. She never visited Kurseong after that and had passed away 13 years later - a couple of years before Parijaat was born.

"How do you know my grandparents this well?" Parijaat asks him.

"We were neighbours," he tells her. "I live in a cottage nearby called Ashoka."

They are at the gate of Ivy Cott, and without a word, Shiv turns around and leaves. From a distance, she hears a voice calling her and then someone gently taps her shoulder.

"Hey! Don't fall asleep here," Rudra tells her, gently nudging her awake. Parijaat realises that she is still at the grotto with Rudra... then what did just happen... was it a dream? She makes her way back to the Ivy Cott with Rudra, wondering if she should tell him about her strange dream.

His presence gives her a sense of calm and grounding. The dream had shaken her a bit. Almost as if rereading her mind, Rudra reaches out for her hand and walks her down to the hotel. His hand feels comforting and… and familiar.

In the evening, Parijaat sits near the bonfire with a peg of whiskey, looking at the intriguing flames. A gentle hand ruffles her hair. It is Rudra, she smiles at him. He pulls up a chair next to her. His scent embraces her and she can almost hear a spark crackle within.

Rudra takes out an old wooden box and shows her several glass bottles containing precious essential oils and attars.

"Would you like to offer feedback on my perfume?" he asks her. Parijaat nods.

In a 10 ML vial, he puts in a drop each of vetiver, patchouli, cedarwood, clary sage and pine essential oils. Rudra swirls the mix and hands over the vial to Parijaat to smell.

He then asks her to smell the oils individually and suggest which one she would like to add more. Cedarwood and pine, she suggests. He adds those, swirls the bottle and gives it to her to sniff again. Their drinks are repeated, the intoxicating warmth of the bonfire adds to the magic of the evening.

Rudra and Parijaat continue their perfume mixing but just something remains missing, and then she looks into his eyes. They are those same haunting brown eyes that she had seen in her hypnotherapy session. She feels faint. Rudra leans towards her and kisses her gently.

At about 2 AM Parijaat returns to her room and before going to bed, she opens her *Complete Volume of John Keats*. Two photographs fall on her lap... one of her... the one that... err... Shiv had taken in the grotto this morning. The other photograph was of her grandmother, at the same place. People say that Parijaat looks just like her grandmother. In the pictures, the only difference is Parijaat is in denim and shirt, and her grandmother is in a saree.

In her sleep, Parijaat hears Shiv's voice.

"Who are you?" she asks.

"Your guiding soul, sweetheart. I waited for you for so many years, you never returned from Kolkata," says Shiv's voice.

Parijaat wakes up at 5 AM again. As she reaches for the water on the desk, she notices Shivnath engraved on it... her grandfather's name was Shivnath... Shiv fondly.

On the desk, she finds a photograph. It's a black and white picture, pretty old and fading but the eyes shine through it. Those eyes that she had seen in her hypnotherapy session. The picture is of Shiv without those thick glasses that he was wearing yesterday.

At the breakfast table, Parijaat asks the duty manager about the Ashoka cottage and the people living there.

"Ashoka cottage... that is in shambles now, no one lives there, Ma'am," he replies.

Just then, Parijaat's phone beeps. It's a message from Rudra. His display picture on the phone, Parijaat realises, is a replica of the black and white photograph of Shiv... Shivnath, her grandfather that she is holding in her hand. Those same dark brown eyes.

Rudra's message reads, "I am at the grotto. I have made the perfume, finally! It just needed a drop of parijaat... parijaat attar... Come over. I am waiting for you."

~~~saudade~~~

Finally, Dev's flight lands in Kolkata after over three hours of delay. Bad weather - that's the reason - a reason that he disagrees with. Rain. Especially, rain in Kolkata can never be 'bad'. As he looks out of the window at the rain-washed city, her smile flashes before his eyes. He quickly closes his eyes to retain that beautiful vision. Dev can smell cloves. She always had a clove in her mouth. He can feel her breath on his neck. The caress of her delicate, slim fingers engaged in his rough, brazen fist. He can hear the tinkling of her laughter - a sound that he hadn't heard in the last 15 years. Since the day he deserted her and this city.

He knows that she still lives here. In some fancy towering apartment near Park Street with her IIT-IIM husband... Why does it bother him?

Did he really think she would wait? Wait for what? Had he given her any reason to? And then he ran away...

He lights a cigarette and releases a circle of smoke through the car window. It's still drizzling. The cab crawls its way through the traffic snarls. He requests the driver to take him via Central Avenue. He agrees reluctantly. But he seems like a pleasant, happy man and hums along with the classic number of Dev Anand, *'Hum Hain Rahi Pyaar Ke'*, playing on Radio

Mirchi. They cross Girish Park. His heart twists. She lived there. He can see her ancestral house. He had spent many evenings standing on this road waiting for her to finally appear at the balcony. He can still feel her embrace. The way she would snuggle her head into a comfortable spot on his chest and let it rest there.

The cab stops at the traffic signal in Chowringhee and immediately a little girl appears at the window with a bunch of jasmine garlands. The smell intoxicates Dev. The enigmatic fragrance of the delicate white blooms that she loved so much. A scent that will always be *her*. In an impulse, he buys the entire bunch from the flower girl. She flashes a big smile and disappears. Immediately he wonders what he will do with these garlands. He decides to go with the flow and wear the garlands around his wrist. It's like her hands holding his wrist. Her touch was neither cool nor warm, just a balance of the two and slightly damp because of her perennial habit of being anxious. They reach The Park hotel.

He places the flowers in a large bowl of water that the housekeeping has provided on request. Dev takes a quick shower. By now the room is languidly fragrant of jasmine. He hunts through his backpack and pulls out the little roll-on bottle that he had got from Goa last week. The perfume surprisingly smelled of her breath.

He wears the blend on his wrist and sets up his laptop and to start working on the manuscript again. A pack of cigarettes, Nusrat on his playlist and a mug of black coffee with a shot of Jack Daniel's and four drops of Honeysuckle Bach Flower Remedy - his companions for this night. Most nights.

It's 5 AM, and he decides to now call it a day. The room still smells of jasmine's last breath. The smell of tobacco seems to decay the lingering notes on his wrist. He feels and smells wasted. He tries to remember how it felt when she tenderly ran her fingers through his hair. As the dawn breaks, he retires to bed.

He wakes up well past noon... almost evening. He quickly showers and goes down to Oxford Bookstore for his book launch. The launch event goes off as planned. Readings from some key passages, answering a few expected questions, book signing, a few posed pictures, some 'candid' shots, clinking of champagne flutes... he quietly slips out. It's pouring in Park Street. He walks down to Kusum Roll Center and then walks up again till Flury's, down Middleton Row, till the tree right in front of the gates of Loreto College. He stands there looking at the gate as he used to two decades ago. Waiting for her to come out of the college gates while being shooed away by the *Darwaan*, Mr Pandey. He would call Dev a stubborn fly - *ziddi makkhi* - returns no matter what.

An old man walks up to him. Oh! That's good old, Mr Pandey. He looks cross, but when he recognises Dev, his face breaks into a smile.

"Aaj kiske liye wait kar raha hai?" he asks him with a wink.

"Usi ke liye," Dev replies back without thinking.

Mr Pandey looks deep into his eyes and informs Dev that now her daughter studies in nursery… she comes to drop and pick her every day. Dev didn't need all this information. He quickly says bye and starts walking back. His eyes start watering. It's a mix of rain and tears. He feels suffocated. His heart feels heavy.

He tumbles into the iconic cake shop, Flury's. Thankfully it doesn't look anything like it used to 20 years ago. He needs something that's not what it used to be. Slowly his nerves settle he orders for a Viennese coffee and a piece of paper. The waiter hands him a notepad. Not bad. His mood changes as he composes these lines…

A Summer In Calcutta

The scent of wet earth,
Refreshes memories of bygone years.

Summer school breaks,

Spent indoors below,
Creaking fans.
Crisp cotton dresses,
Slowly sticking to the skin.
Languid lunches,
Followed by afternoon siestas.
Those were times,
When devouring mangoes and lychees,
Was never a guilt or crime.

It still isn't,
After all how can you,
Count calories,
In a city where at every turn,
You will find,
Chop, cutlet, shingara,
Kochuri, roll and jhilipi?

Romance and nostalgia,
Flows through the streets.
In book stores and restaurants,
Lost lovers seek,
Their beloved Bela Bose,
While Anjan Dutta strums,
His classic at Someplace Else next door.

At sunset, in their hearts,
They still haunt the Outram Ghat,
Fleetingly remembering the days,
Spent walking in the rains.

Today from their glass cabins,
They still look out at the,
Season's first shower,
And with a smile,
Fondly remember their first lover.
This memory is enough,
To drive one to Peter Cat,
Where over Bloody Mary,
And Chelo Kebab,
Yesterday is revisited.

With a satiated heart,
One walks down Park Street.
Gets soaked in the rain,
With a promise to repeat this again.

Around 9:30 PM he makes his way back to the hotel and then enters Someplace Else. Is this for real? Anjan Dutta is actually singing tonight, and the moment Dev settles in, Dutta sings 'Bela Bose'. It's such a predictable song... Dev's heart cries out for her momentarily. He feels embarrassed and returns to his room and his playlist of Nusrat. He sits in his room and listens to *"Yeh Jo Halka Halka Suroor Hai"* while looking at the rain outside the window.

He wakes up at noon, freshens up and walks down to Oxford Bookstore for a meeting. He is requested to sign a book for the host of today's event at the store. It's the launch of a book of fragrances. Dev is invited to be a part of it. He says with disdain, "I am happy to partake the wine and wish the debutante author the very best from my corner at the Cha Bar. Not interested in going through this gimmick." The organisers retreat. Who likes spending time with an arrogant man? And that's precisely what he wanted them to do. Disappear.

An hour later, he can hear the set up begin. Chairs being drawn, mikes getting tested, books being arranged... He decides to take a quick walk down Park Street.

By the time he returns, the event is in full swing. He finds himself a discreet corner. He can hear glasses being passed around and then a familiar voice says,

"Near, far, wherever you are, Calcutta is a city that always, somehow induces nostalgia for itself, its people, its culture, its food, its bygone days and more... When I think of my city of birth, the aromas that come to my mind are that of jasmine, sandalwood and neroli. Caressing and loving these notes are like a balm for the soul. And that's the composition of my perfume, Saudade. Please open the lid labelled Saudade and inhale."

Dev almost spills the tea. It is her. It is her voice. It is Kady. It is Kadambari...

He can now see her from where he is sitting. She looks as elegant and fresh as she looked the day he had first seen her. She was wearing an inky blue salwar kameez and laughing with her friends. She always laughed throwing her head back and her eyes closing for a moment and then opening with a sparkle. Today she is wearing a similar inky blue saree. The chiffon *pallu*, pinned at one end of her shoulder, gently flows down her slim arms. Dev can almost feel that soft fabric on his arm.

She looks a bit tense and unsure. Her eyes scan the audience, looking for something... someone.

Nostalgia unleashes itself in Dev's heart. Kadambari was always a shy, timid girl. Their romance had bloomed despite severe opposition from her home. She would often speak of marriage but it would terrify Dev. Just to keep her heart, he went and met her parents. It was a disaster. He had planned it to be one. He was duly rejected, and he was elated. But her sad face broke his heart. She tried convincing her family. She fought for Dev but by then he was not there for her. He tried various ways of getting away. His shirt clung to his skin, heavy with her tears and his sweat. And then he finally told her on her face that he wanted to end it. She just said one sentence, "If I go away today, I will walk away forever." Dev ran away to Oxford. To get his mind off her for a while and perhaps come back to her later. But within a year she got married. She did walk away forever.

He looks at her again. A man walks up the stairs. Seeing him, her face lights up. Her tension eases and she takes people through the session with sparkling elegance. Though Dev can't see this man's face yet, he has no doubt about who he is. He can see the love that she has for him in her eyes. She is madly in love with him. But only one who knows her will realise it. A wine sample is being passed around for tasting as she reads out a poem that she has composed:

In Thunder and Rain

The rain melts on the window pane,
The wind knocks on the gate.
The sky lights up for a moment,
And the thunder makes its presence felt.

What message do the clouds bring today?
Is it a promise for tomorrow?
Or an unfinished tale of the past?

A streak of lightning connects all at once,
In a flash clarity appears.
It fades away in a moment,
But in that moment you have lived and loved.

Words remain at the tongue tip,

Questions get swallowed within.
Only a smile is left behind,
When you call it a night.

As she wraps up the session, she is presented with Dev's book. He had quickly inserted a note in it before it was taken for her. He can now see her opening the book and reading the note.

Dev had written, "I am sorry, Kady. But you are the only woman I have ever loved..." She smiles, folds the note and holds it in her hand and walks up to her husband. As she stands there, she gently stirs the note into the bowl of water with jasmine flowers.

The organiser of the event comes up to Dev with her book that had just been released. It was signed by her, and it had a little note that said,

"We of those times, no longer the same."

~~~vibhatsu - the deathly fear~~~

"This is the fourth time in a month, doctor," he said. "It keeps coming. I can't sleep."

Dr Ronipa Das studied him before thinking of a reply. He was disturbed. His eyes were searching for something but scared. The potholes around his eyes were more visible than the last time he visited here. His lips were restless. They were shivering. He kept on wetting them with his tongue. He was rubbing his palms with each other. His legs were equally restless.

"What exactly did you see this time?" Dr Das finally opened her mouth.

"The same, the same..." he shook his head, "the hilltop, the cliff, the deep land beneath, a rough flowing river and a monster calling me down there..." his voice trembled a bit. "It's horrible!" He said after a pause.

"And?"

"And that voice," he wailed, "that scary voice that drives me mad and takes away my sleep."

"Is it the voice of the monster?" Dr Das asked him.

"I don't know." He further said, "Doctor, please do something. I'm going to die..."

"Arjun, you are absolutely healthy. You are not going to die."

"I'm afraid of death. That voice reminds me always that my time is over."

"It's just a dream. It's a nightmare."

The fear of death was visible on his face. He was so scared that he couldn't sit properly.

"Here, drink water." Dr Das slid the glass of water to him. He gently grabbed it and took a sip from it. Dr Das spoke up again,

"Arjun, I know you for a long time. You already have insomnia. You hallucinate often. This might be a part of all that. I'm giving you a medici..."

"No!" Arjun shouted, "I am not hallucinating."

"After your parent's death, you felt yourself alone all the time. You are not even close to your uncle who brought you up. You don't talk to anyone much. Your psychological problem has a reason, Arjun. Try mixing up with people. Talk to them. Make friends."

"You don't understand. I tried all of these. But death is following me everywhere." Arjun murmured, "Somebody wants to kill me."

"Why will somebody wants to kill you?"

"I don't know." He put his head down on the table. Dr Das took a deep breath.

"Arjun, go home."

"Oh," he lifted his head.

"Your session time is over."

He looked at his watch and said, "No."

Dr Das smiled, "Umm...yes. I have to go home too."

"Good night, doctor." He left the seat. His six feet tall figure unwillingly proceeded towards the chamber's door.

"Good night." Dr Das' face turned serious. This is the strangest case in her 10 years of career as a psychiatrist.

Why does Arjun think that somebody will kill him? Just because of a scary voice and an imaginary monster?

Arjun, at twenty-seven, has his own house, car, money, and a lot of hobbies. He is a trained guitarist, a skilful footballer, and a voracious reader and researcher of English literature. He lost his parents 21 years ago. His mother died of cancer in June 1999, and his father died of an accident in September in the same year.

His uncle brought him up. Later after passing school, he started living alone in a separate house.

Arjun had come to Dr Das three years ago. He came with a severe problem of insomnia. Later, she discovered that he hallucinated when he told her that he could see his parents in his room. His treatment continued for two years. Dr Das is Arjun's emergency contact since then. He still suffers from insomnia but now what?

Dr Das couldn't come up with a conclusion. It was hallucination or dream? She went home thinking of him all the way.

Arjun was afraid of death. He never knew that he had to fear something like death. How easily people ignore the fact that they all have to die and death is the only certain thing in life that moves like an umbrella with every mortal. And when they think of it, they come to a psychiatrist.

He went home and collapsed on the couch. His head twisted. His eyes were sore. He could see nothing but darkness. Suddenly he experienced a free fall. His eyes shot open, and his heart started beating hard. He jumped out of the couch. But he was not alone. He felt someone's presence in the room.

"Who's there?" his voice cracked.

He heard a voice, "Death."

He stepped back, but he could not reach the couch. He tripped over something on the dark floor. He tried to get up fighting against a new and unknown force.

A black veil approached him.

"Please… I don't want to die." Arjun's voice pleaded. It was not just fear anymore. It was an urge to live.

"Arjun." The hoarse, scary voice said again.

"Go away!" Arjun's urge of living grew stronger.

"Arjun, get up. It's me, Dr Das."

He suddenly felt his eyes burning. The light from the windows hurt his eyes. He sat up quickly and looked around to find Dr Das standing beside him.

"Where am I?" he asked.

"In my house," Dr Das said. "Last night, your maid informed me that you didn't reach home. She was very scared. I went out to search for you. Luckily, I found you near my chamber."

"What?" he couldn't believe it. His heart was still racing against everything around him.

"How did I go there?"

"Don't you remember anything from last night?"

"No." He shook his head. The sign of strain on his forehead was clearly visible. "I thought I was home."

"Are you sure that you are taking your medicines properly?" Dr Das asked.

"I don't know anything." He cried helplessly. "I have a heavy head. It's difficult for me to hold my head up."

"You are not into drugs, right?" she almost whispered to him.

He looked at her face, "You already got me a test last time, and it was negative."

"Yes," She nodded. She passed a coffee mug to him. He grabbed it gently and stared at it for a long time.

Dr Das was observing her patient, carefully.

"Whom were you asking to go away?" she asked after some time.

"Hmm?" he was lost somewhere. He came back to reality by the doctor's question. "Death," he answered. "He came in a black veil."

"He?"

"It can be 'she' as well," Arjun said, looking at her. "I don't know. But I saw it closely." His voice shook while saying the last sentence.

"How does it look like?"

"Scary. Horrible. Faceless," he said.

She remained quiet. This was the strangest thing she heard in her whole career. Arjun stared back at his coffee.

"Do you know that the other name of Arjun is Vibhatsu?"

He looked up at her with a curl on his forehead. "Oh… that Arjun. Yes. I know." He said after some time and looked back to his coffee.

"Impressive. What does it mean?"

"I don't know." He was sitting like before and answering softly.

"Gruesome. Fearsome." She said, walking around the room gathering her hands at her back. "He, whom, even the fear has feared to face. Arjun was called Vibhatsu because he had overcome his fears in fighting in the war. He was so powerful to do what he was supposed to do without fearing anything or anyone."

He stayed quiet.

"The best way to escape from the deathly fear is to overcome it – to win over it."

"How?" he asked softly placing his coffee mug on the table. The absolutely cold coffee rested lifelessly.

"After your parents' death in front of your eyes, death has become your biggest fear, Arjun. You have to win over it."

"How?" he shouted impatiently. "Tell me a damn way. How do I get rid of that dream?"

"There's always a way, Arjun. But I am not finding one for this now," she said. "Stay at my home until everything gets fine."

The last sentence was unexpected to him.

Two days passed like that. Arjun couldn't rest. He couldn't eat properly, he couldn't sleep. Not even with the help of medicines and therapies. Dr Das kept on thinking about Arjun's dream. What's the treatment for this? Her complete knowledge of psychology was failing in front of this.

'He has a deathly fear.' She whispered to herself sometimes.

The next morning she found Arjun sitting on the floor of the balcony. He was aimlessly wondering at the sky.

"Hey, had a nice sleep?" she asked him.

He just smirked.

"We are going to explore a place today." She said in an informative way to him.

He looked at her, "We?"

"You and me," she smiled at him.

"Where?"

"Somewhere I know."

"Is this a part of my treatment?"

"Maybe." She said, proceeding towards the bathroom.

Two hours later, they were on the extreme end of the city. This is one of those picturesque hills located in the north of the town.

Arjun found him standing at the end of a cliff. It went deep down, straight to the river that flows roughly like a violent beast. His heart jumped up in fear. It was the same place he dreamt of. His face lost its colour.

"Is there a monster?" Dr Das' voice scared him even more.

"How do you know about this place?" he cried, stepping back. "It's the same place..." he screamed. "Please take me home." He almost caught her feet, pleading for life.

"It's the same place where you saw your dad dying." Dr Das spoke up. "He fell down the cliff, drunk driving. You saw this place because your uncle was following him to stop him from going at the extreme end of the cliff. You were in the passenger seat of your uncle's car. Your uncle couldn't save your father because he was drunk, sad about your mother's death. He was not in his senses and drove directly to the peak."

Arjun was just listening.

"It started coming to you after all these years as a tragic memory, then as a dream, or nightmare, whatever you like to call it."

Arjun was sweating badly in his pullover. His face still had no colour.

"Childhood tragedies come back as the biggest fear of life, Arjun," she said. "Your biggest fear is death because you saw two deaths closely at a young age. The black veil you saw is nothing but your illustration of death. The monster is nothing but the falling car you saw from the cliff going down to the river."

"How did you know all these?" he asked now.

"I am a psychiatrist," Dr Das said. "A bad one indeed. I didn't study your case carefully. Last night I called your uncle and got to know how your dad died when I narrated him your dream."

Arjun stood up gently and moved to the extreme edge of the cliff. Everything started to come to him. The racing car, the screech of the tire, his uncle pleading to stop his father, he – sitting on his uncle's car, crying.... and then the accident... or suicide... or whatever it was... his father went far away from him... His heart raced faster. His breath became more frequent.

"Death is so easy, right?" he smirked, "just a fall from here to reach there," he laughed.

"Yes, death is so easy. It's just a veil between this cliff and that river, down there."

Arjun laughed more.

"Vibhatsu..." he kept on laughing. "I was afraid of this veil? Just a veil..."

Dr Das saw him with patience and silence.

"Death seems so casual. So powerless," he said. "Vibhatsu... Vibhatsu..." he kept on saying.

Then he burst out laughing again. He laughed so hard that his eyes turned moist.

He turned to Dr Das, "Can we go home? Can I rest?" he almost pleaded. "I'm so sleepy."

"Sure." Dr Das extended to hold his hand, smiling widely.

~~~the last leaf~~~

"Ammi!" cries Sheela and says, "Kishore is cheating in the game again." She runs inside the house to her mother, who was cooking evening snacks in the kitchen for the family. With sweat running on her face like a redhandedly caught criminal, her mother smiles and shake at her. It's nothing unusual for the kids to have a fight while playing together. Sheela tucks on her mother's saree and repeatedly keeps saying, "I am not going to play with him anymore. He is a cheater. He always cheats and can never play a fair game."

While she is complaining, Kishore smirks and says, "Ammi, I never cheat. She is just a cry baby." Kishore looks at her sister and asks her to stop creating a fuss. "Even I am not interested in playing with you. You're such a whiner."

The kids' father returns from his jewellery shop, meanwhile. He enters the home and is welcomed by the sounds of squabble of his children. Sheela exclaims 'papa' and runs to hug and greet her father, who then picks his little daughter in his arms and gently pats his son. He asks Sheela, "Who has been troubling my princess? Is it your naughty brother?" Sheela quickly nods in agreement as she senses the opportunity to avenge the feeling of humiliation she felt at being called a whiner. His father gives Kishore a darn look and warns him not to trouble her sister. Instead, he should be protective of her.

The mother fetches a glass of water for her husband, who has just arrived and busied himself with the little ones. "Who wants to eat this tasty malai bread now?" she asks. Both the kids shout joyously at the thought of having a delicious evening snack. The mother instructs them both to wash their faces and hands first. Both go away quickly.

While sipping evening tea with bread and biscuits, the mother informs her husband of collecting kids' results between eight in the morning and noon of the upcoming day. Sheela studies in eighth grade in an all-girls school while Kishore, in an all-boys school. Both the schools were near to their house.

Each morning Kishore and Sheela leave the house together. Kishore would drop Sheela first to her school gate and then proceed towards his school. The next morning they both get dressed in their school uniforms as they would on a regular day. Sheela wears a white suit paired with an equally plain white salwar, which she hated because of the lack of beautiful colours, only because she once saw a girl from another school who had a colourful school uniform. Kishore wears a crisp white shirt and knee-length navy blue shorts and a blue striped tie. They go to Sheela's school first, and their eyes filled with the joys of spring when her teacher told them that she ranked first in the class. Then they go to Kishore's school with a wave of optimism that was short-lived. Kishore had scored a meagre 40% which wasn't very pleasing after all. Sheela doesn't tease her brother, instead encourages him to study harder. Siblings are the best friends and worst enemies, Kishore thinks. To celebrate, Sheela goes to the railway station in the evening with a friend to eat onion fritters which are frowned upon in her family as onions are forbidden in the Hindu Brahmin family. She doesn't feel guilty as she thinks she deserves to eat those. In the times where hardly any importance is given to educating a girl child with the mentality that she should learn only household chores to become a good wife, Sheela wants to go to college in Lahore after completing her school education. Her father agrees to her wish of studying in a city which is somewhat far from where they live. The day-to-day activities keep them busy for the next two years.

One evening, her father returns from his jewellery shop with looks of despair and hopelessness. He tells his wife about the rumours of the partition of the nation into Hindu and Muslim territories.

His wife says, "Don't worry. It's all politicians-aided trivial fight. The fire in these anguished men will be extinguished soon."

Sheela insists that it is her last year at school and they would have a class photograph the next day. Despite the refusal from her parents, she goes to her school all dressed in a pretty colourful red suit-salwar, while all the others present wore regular suits. There are disturbances in the entire neighbourhood and nation. There is news of violence, mass murders and loot all across the country. Her father being a jeweller, has contacts in the now Indian part. Somehow, the family of four escapes the city amidst all the stories of horrors of violence where Hindus were being tortured, killed, and women were assaulted sexually. They manage to take some of their gold and cash essential for survival. It is a tough journey.

They live in refugee tents. Sheela ponders about the contrast in her life from being the daughter of a wealthy jeweller, living in a large mansion with a beautiful garden in the front to living in a refugee tent with limited supplies. She would sometimes read a book under the dim light in those refugee tents. She likes reading poetry and novels. Though they teach English for only two years in her school, Sheela develops a good command over the language. She loves gazing at the stars and moon in the night sky and somehow relates the night sky to her own life. Her life is dark, though it is illuminated by the stars and the moon - her parents and brother. The realization of being safe with her family calms her in these troubling times. She has seen people in worse conditions in the camps and has heard the news that would make her shiver. She is grateful to God for keeping her family close. She always has this undying optimism in herself even in the darkest times of her life.

One day, as she was sky gazing at night time, a man appeared near her. He said that she should avoid staying outside the tent at such odd hours. She ignored him more out of fear rather than any ill-mannered teenager. The old man's face was more glowing than the other people of his age. He asked the little girl to stretch her hand towards him as he had a gift for her. The man said, "I am giving you a treasure. Plant these seeds when you have a child. It will give your child a wonderful life. But remember the last leaf on this tree will mark your last breath on this Earth." Sheela took the seeds and kept them inside the little purse she carried. Before she could look upwards again, the man disappeared into thin air. She looked around for him, but he was nowhere in sight. She was shocked about what just happened. She believed it was just a cheap antic. Though a part of her believed in it firmly and the other part refused to acknowledge it at all. She wanted to reveal this incident to someone. However, she knew her parents would scold her and hardly believe her. They would think of it as a make-believe story.

As days passed, she started thinking less about this incident. Soon, they moved to a house from those refugee tents. Her mother passed away in her sleep one night. Years after, Sheela got married to a guy running a business in another city. He mostly stayed away and rarely came home to spend time with her. She thought that the fate of all women is to sit at home. They exchanged letters some times. Sheela would pass her time at home with her in-laws. Although after two years, the whole marriage turned into a scam when she decided to give a surprise visit to her husband working in the other city and found him living with another woman. As much as Sheela wanted to burst in tears, the shock couldn't let her do so and made her leave without saying a word. She also found that he concealed his actual age.

Moreover, having a drunkard husband isn't the wish of any woman. Her husband died after a year because of liver failure. She had nowhere to go and was left all alone. She didn't want to trouble her father with her sorrows. While she was packing her stuff, she noticed the small purse in which she had those seeds. She thought of that night and started thinking about her childhood days, considering those the best time of her life as she could have anything in the world by just asking her parents. Kishore encouraged her to remarry, which was contrary to what their father wanted.

Kishore got Sheela married to a cousin of his wife. He wasn't wealthy but belonged to a well to do family. He was educated and open-minded. He had an aura of beaming positivity around him that lured Sheela. Her new husband had an elder brother and his wife besides his parents. Within a few months of marriage, she realized that her mother-in-law and sister-in-law weren't very approving of her and would rather treat her in improper ways of mannerism. At first, she thought it was her being a remarried widow, but then she discovered as her husband was financially weaker than his brother, the love of a mother could be uneven. Till then, she thought that mothers only love their sons more than daughters. But this was new to her. Though the love of her husband helped her ignore that and move past all family drama. Moreover, she believed her spirituality was actually serving her as a support system.

Sheela had a childhood habit of reading at bedtime. Her new husband asked, "What makes you so interested in reading?" to which she replied, "It makes me more accepting of the people around me." Her husband understood her thirst for the need to comprehend life as a philosopher. She also told her husband that she wants a peaceful death somewhere near the trees reading a book. Her husband laughed and said, "Who thinks about death? We have got all life ahead of us, and you are already making plans for death?"

They both eventually fell in love with each other, and soon Sheela got pregnant. They were so excited at the thought of becoming parents. Her mother-in-law asked her, "So are you giving birth to a boy or an abortion?" This was a deep-rooted superiority complex in the mother of two boys, and the rest could be blamed on the society's way of treating women.

During her fourth month, the doctor said that the child has a deformity, and the only viable solution was abortion. The news troubled both Sheela and her husband. Her husband claimed it was because of the stupid things his mother said the other day that God won't endow his blessings to them for having a child now. Sheela said, "We shouldn't blame her unnecessarily. It is not pleasant news, but no one should be blamed for such uncontrollable things." That night Sheela couldn't sleep. She kept tossing and turning. Even gazing at the night sky couldn't calm her racing thoughts filled with fear of loss of her first child. Just about dawn, like Archimedes, she had her moment of Eureka. She remembered about the seeds that the old man had given to her. Just about the crack of dawn, she began to frantically search for that purse. She found it and thought it was the perfect moment to try if what the old man said was true or just an antic like she felt at that time. She planted the seeds that morning in the garden that was visible from her room and decided to keep it to herself to avoid being mocked just like the earlier times.

A week passed, and the couple went to the hospital. To their surprise, the doctor told them that it is a miracle that the child's body had automatically aligned the bone that caused the deformity. Sheela was happy, more than any words could describe. She had a wave of faith and calmness running in her body. She told her husband that because of this happiness and positive news, she planted some seeds in the garden. A few months after, Sheela gave birth to a beautiful baby girl. As she grew up, the little girl always awaited to hear the bedtime stories from her mother. She developed a reading habit just like her mother. The little girl was fascinated by the life of people abroad. The childhood dream became her adulthood ambition. However, when she had to go to college, Sheela's brother-in-law would ask them to get her admission in some college which has low fees or any small course. Sheela always understood the importance of education. She always thought that she missed college due to the unfortunate events at that time. But that must not stop her daughter from gaining an education. Sheela would allow her daughter to explore life and find new paths.

The little seeds had also grown to become a big tree in all these years. Sheela always smiled and thanked the tree and the old man. With the help of educational loans, Sheela's daughter completed her post-graduation. Finally, she received a job offer to work overseas. She got a chance to live her dream. Her parents were proud of her achievements. She moved to Australia to work with a big corporation. As time went by, they heard less and less from her. Few years passed, and Sheela's husband died of a heart attack. Now Sheela was left all alone. Her husband's pension took care of her needs and expenses. She kept looking at the 'magical' tree from her room while she lay in the bed. She was always cheerful and would distribute toffees to the neighbourhood children as they gathered almost every evening to hear a story from the old lady who still had clear speech and exciting stories. The tree had started to shed its leaves, and the more leafless it became, the more lifeless Sheela felt. There were just last few leaves left on the branches of the tree.

Another evening, she was sitting in her garden on a rocking chair, enjoying the light breeze, gathered by four of the neighbourhood children. She read a story to them, and they left. It was late evening by then. The sun was going out of sight. She then finished her cup of tea and picked up a poetry book. It was a collection of classic poems. She opened a random page on the poetry of Dylan Thomas, and the first two lines read, "Do not go gentle into the night, Old age should burn and rave at the close of the day." As she read this, she saw the last leaf on the tree, making its way to the ground. In her final moments, the face and the words of the old man kept flashing in her mind. She took a deep breath, knowing it would be her last. She kept the book on her chest, smiled and closed her eyes forever.

~~~**troubled**~~~

My head ached severely. I felt as if someone had hurt it with a heavy weapon. My face was roughly bandaged for several cuts and wounds. I couldn't move. My numb hands were unable to clutch a single thing lying in front of me. A mixed aroma of several medicines was pestering my nostrils tremendously. I didn't understand where I actually was until I opened my blurry eyes. God damn! I was lying in a hospital bed. A noise of other patients, nurses, and on-duty doctors was truly annoying. My wrist-veins were pricked with several injections for the circulation of saline. I had no strength to utter a single word. My bed was placed beside a window. I efforted enough to reach the window sills, opened them for the fresh air to brush my face directly but a swarm of questions stung on my brain instead of the freshness.

'Who am I? What do I do? Where do I belong?' I had no answers to these questions. I felt like I am lost in an ocean of nothingness. I never felt so worthless in my life. I wanted to shriek like an insane beggar, but nothing came into my rescue. Suddenly I saw a nurse approaching towards me with her hands crammed with medicines, needles, and medicinal stuff. She smiled, came and asked, "How are you feeling now?"

I was clueless about what I should say. I said, "I don't know how I am feeling. My head is paining heavily. I am not able to think properly."

She gestured with her hand for me to calm down and said, "You don't have to pressurize your brain, Mister. We are here to take care of you. Let's just get a little better first."

I couldn't resist my urge to know my details and asked, "Sister, can you please tell me who I am? And how am I here? Because I forgot everything. I am feeling so unworthy now."

She prevented me from breaking down and said, "Don't worry. Everything will be fine. We are trying to work on your identification. We are even in touch with the nearby police station to help us out. Two days ago, we found you outside our hospital. You were badly wounded, and there were several cuts in your whole body. We took you here in an emergency condition and went through an operation. That's it."

I promptly said, "Please tell me the name of this hospital and the area."

She replied, "Apollo Centre of Medicine, St. Lewis Road, Park Street."

I was just going to thank her when she said, "Well, there is one more thing we need to acknowledge you about. We got a small note from your pocket. Thought of handing it over to you. Please take this."

She handed me over a small note and went for the next patient. I was bombarded with surprises one after another. I opened the crumpled note, the message was, 'Do not try to mess with me. Otherwise, you will be doomed again. Hahaha.'

This gave me several goosebumps, I could feel my heavy breath, and I was sweating like hell. I never felt such fear in my life ever. I felt my presence was a tug of war where I was dangling in an existential crisis.

For the next seven days, I laid in the bed like a still object. I was under acute observation of doctors. The food felt tasteless, and even the water didn't give satisfaction.

After seven days, I tried to get up from the bed and walk a little. I was strolling through the corridor on the second floor of the hospital. Just in a few days, the hospital staff became so cordial that they gave me a warm smile when I passed by. I was standing beside the railing, resting my elbows on them and enjoying the charm of nature when suddenly something hit my arm. I was startled. I noticed that a piece of note wrapped in a small stone was thrown at me. I picked it up and what I read, blanked my head.

'Don't try to be over smart. Else, you will be killed. If you want to know who you are, meet me tomorrow at 12 PM sharp at Atlas Building, Subidhi Street. Bye. Hahaha.'

A stroke of wild wind slushed me with turbulence in my mind. I was scared and curious to know everything at the same time. I fixed my mind that I needed to head there tomorrow to reveal all the mysteries. As per my plan, I managed the hospital authority to grant me a leave for tomorrow.

Apocalypse wasn't far, so as the next day. As per my preparation, I borrowed a dress and some money from a ward-boy and got out of the hospital at sharp 11 AM. I forgot everything about this city, so I booked a taxi and told him to take me towards Atlas Building, Subidhi Street. As the taxi-driver drove towards the location, my heartbeat increased. And finally, I reached the location.

Subidhi Street was a long hushed street. There were a lot of abandoned buildings on both sides of the road. Getting out of the taxi, I searched for Atlas Building here and there. I kept walking straight and then paused. I was feeling terrible just when again I got a crumpled note collided with my shoulder. Again I opened it, and it said, "Walk straight and then you will find the building at the end of the street. Catch the stairs and get up. A lot more is awaiting!"

I followed the instruction, walked and finally found the horrendous looking building at the end. My hands trembled, sweated and turned numb. I entered the almost-collapsed building. I took the stairs and went up. Screeching darkness prevailed here and there.

I couldn't see anything properly. I might have entered a room. A sudden push knocked me down to the floor, followed by a kick on my knee.

Terror trickled down my spine, I shouted, "Who are hell are you? Answer me right now."

A loud roll of laughter ringed the whole room. The other voice answered, "I am someone who brought a nightmare to your life, Mister Deviprasad. Do not forget I am the hunter, and you are the prey. Hahahaha."

I was unable to lift up my frail body, I laid on the ground, and the name from his mouth sounded so familiar. My head was burning in confusion. I replied, "For God's sake, do not play with me like this, you bastard. Just tell me the truth and everything."

Suddenly He lit up a lighter and came very close to me. Bald head, fair complexion, dark eyebrows, intense round eyes, a short cut from the corner of the left eye touched till the middle of his flat nose, brown moustache, and a sly smile from the edge of his thick lips were transparent in front of me. I was raging in anger. Rapidly I tried to slap him, but he caught my hand in the blink of an eye. Taking me in roll, he moved across the ground. We were jostling with each other. A round of physical wrestling was highly reigning on. I thumped him, and he reverted back with two on my face. Blood splashed from my lips. I had no strength to face him in such a condition. He thumped on my belly one more time. I was gasping. I was tracing for a way to save myself. Amidst all these, he laughed like a demon, saying,

"Deviprasad, I wanted to kill you that day but couldn't accomplish my plan. Your bloody wife and son came into my path. I killed them too. But you, lucky fellow, were mercied from my trap. No matter what, I will fulfil my desire today right now."

His words went through my body like an electric shock. I was tattered hearing I had a wife and a son, and they were dead too. I cursed myself for more than ever. I shrieked,

"You, the son of a bitch, killed my family too. How dare you? Oh God, kill me too. I do not wish to live anymore."

I howled like a helpless when his loud laughter destroyed my ears. He said,

"I am so happy to see you shattered. Now you deserve to know my name. I am Mr Michael Gonsalves. The one whom you put behind bars for seven years. You bloody lawyer, you spoiled my seven years from my life. Now, Michael will snatch your life. Hahaha."

He was just galloping along with me with a sharp knife when the door of the room banged.

A group of five cops, pointing their guns shouted, "Hands up! Nobody will move. Or else, we would shoot."

Michael's attention shattered, his hands quivered, and the knife from his hand fell off on the ground. Two cops caught him from behind, and he was trying his best to escape from their grips.

The Inspector came towards me, helped me get up and held me saying,

"Sir, Deviprasad Thakur, we got to know everything from the Apollo Centre of Medicine. We are investigating your case for the past week. We were just going to the hospital to meet you and tell you everything about your identification and your accident. When we reached there, we heard that you were out for an hour. We got shocked, and as per the information from the ward-boy Ajit, we came here. Sir, we are really sorry that we reached really late and you faced such assault from this rogue."

He turned away and slapped restless Michael. He commanded other cops to take him to the police jeep. The last time Michael gave me a horrendous look and left the place saying, "I shall see you, Mr Deviprasad. I shall see you soon…"

The Inspector again moved towards me, smiled a little and said, "Come, we would drop you to the hospital."

I asked, "Can you please explain to me those I forgot? I need to know everything as soon as possible. I am losing my brain. It hurts my heart severely."

He persuaded and said, "Sir, you need rest. We shall let you know everything when you will be fine physically. Let's go from this place."

He tucked my hand carefully and took me along with him. We left the place, boarded on his jeep. As we were passing the roads, some thoughts brushed their faces on my mind. Just half an hour ago, I was in the firm grip of my worst enemy and now was saved.

'Will I ever be able to find my true belonging? Will I ever be able to trace my scars and get back my life?' Such questions dabbed my soul.

My name 'Deviprasad Thakur' felt like the first clue to solving all the riddles of my life. Inspector looked at me and smiled. I smiled too, but I was not happy. I smiled because I appreciated the whole scenario that dragged me towards a solution. The jeep stopped as we reached the hospital. The staffs were waiting outside anxiously to see me. They took a long breath watching me alive. I bade adieu to the Inspector, and he waved goodbye too. I looked at the sky, maybe in search of a ray of hope.

Everything has a solution, so have life. Troubled now. Solved tomorrow.

~~~so what?~~~

'Life is a joke, and all things show it
I thought so once, but now I know it.'

I had read this anonymous poem in school and wondered how someone could be so totally detached. Ignoring all the confusion, all the pain, all that wretched feeling of being used by ungrateful friends, to believe that life is a joke and laugh about it. But someone had said it and said it in rhyme, for which I have a special place in my scheme of things.

Till I met Surekha. This is an ancient story dating back to 1972, my first year in MA at Delhi University. I was putting up a hand- made poster in the Arts Faculty, inviting all my classmates to attend a seminar in my Hindu College. That was the only way to grab the attention of the girls from Miranda and Lady Sriram College (LSR). We could not match the Stephanians (whom we referred to as coming from the college across the road) showing off their flashing cameras and bikes without silencers.

My plan worked, and a quietly beautiful girl from LSR, dressed in pink matching her complexion walked up to me, saying, "You have not mentioned the time of the seminar in your poster."

Excited as a child who had just mastered the Pythagoras theorem I thanked her for pointing it out, hoping that she would make it. However, all my primal passion cooled off as she replied matter-of-factly, "Sorry, it is not about me. I can't make it as I have to catch my University U-Special, but I thought that those who did want to come would be inconvenienced."

I thought I had noticed a faint smile on her bright face with those fluttering eyes as if she had made a kill. Most likely, it was my imagination going wild.

PS: This story dates back to a period when the Metro had not come to Delhi.

After this introduction, she just breezed into my existence so naturally. Whenever we got together for the class, our eyes met involuntarily and without saying a word she would drift away from her friends, including her best friend Shashi whom I knew before her, and quietly come and sit down with me before the class began. In any case, attendance was not compulsory in MA English, and it was entirely up to us whether we wanted to sit inside the class or sit on the walls outside to listen to the lectures.

One day she came an hour before the class, and we (yes, just the two of us) headed towards the Coffee Home across the Arts Faculty as if by some prior understanding.

As we savoured a steaming cup of coffee in the balmy winter morning of December, I said, "Thanks for coming early all the way from Hauz Khas to spend time together."

"Oh, hello! I came early because my U-Special comes early. I can't travel in crowded buses with uncouth passengers staring and trying to touch me," said Surekha. "These *chaloo* men. Don't they get a chance to get cosy with their wives at home or what?" She grimaced.

I put my head down. Feeling ashamed for the whole species of men. Till I heard her complimenting someone who had just entered the coffee shop, muttering almost under her breath, "That's a lovely saree."

The shapely stranger who was walking out in a hurry stopped in her tracks (which woman on earth does not have time to take compliments) and flashed a huge smile, "Thank you."

It was Surekha's turn to look embarrassed, "Oh, you heard me" and turned beet-root red from her usually pink visage. Which suited her perfectly as she was herself dressed in a parrot green saree, which is not easy to carry for normal girls.

But this was the essential Surekha. Showering compliments at anything/anyone she liked and pointing out any error or gesture her kajal-painted shining eyes noticed. So casually, and yet making the adrenaline rush at a furious speed in my system.

The other day we were walking towards the Hindu College library when I involuntarily jumped up to pluck a flower from a tree. But before I could present it to her, she winked at me impishly, saying, "Oh, you were waving at her," looking at a girl who had just passed us but not close enough to hear this unexpected compliment.

I had no idea when my life became so incomplete without her till we had a four-day vacation before Dewali. I even wrote a poem defining my life as 'a circle without a centre' when I did not see her.

On the third day, I picked up some library books and reached her house unannounced because mobiles had not been invented by that time, and even landline phones were a luxury. I was considered the most studious of our group of four Surekha, Shashi, Ajay and myself and this alibi of books always worked.

As soon as I rang the bell she was at the door nonchalantly with that 'I knew it' victory smile. No, we didn't hug in those times, and it did not occur to us to even touch each other, not even when alone in a movie hall. She waved at me to follow her and introduced me to her mother and sister.

It was the first time that I came to know after about ten months of studying together that they were just three of them in the family. Her father was living separately in someplace no one wanted to talk about? But we never discussed this ever again as she tried to avoid the pain associated with those ghosts from her childhood.

Shashi and Surekha used to take a lift back home every day. Obviously, I was jealous and taunted them about it. Shashi, who was the conscience keeper of our group and Surekha's fierce guardian, told me that it was not easy.

"There are certain rules we have to follow. If a vehicle stops to give us a lift, the normal principle is that we ask them which way they were going. If it is on our route, we get in. Even if we have to change two or three times. If the fellow tries to oblige us by offering to change the route, it is a strict No-No," she explained.

One day Shashi and Surekha invited me to join them on one of these adventures as they headed home after class. I stood with them on the pavement, but Shashi pushed me back.

"Don't stand here for God's sake. No one will stop to give us a lift if they see you. When we have stopped a car come out from behind that wall," she suggested.

"And then if he refuses he's had it," I growled.

Surekha was enjoying this adventure more than she had planned. After two cars had passed us, a shining Ambassador stopped, and as the driver opened the front gate of the car, Surekha called out my name. The driver's face grew crimson as he reluctantly opened the car for me. I dared not look into the rear mirror throughout the one hour journey, but it was great fun, chuckling at his discomfiture.

From our group, it was Ajay who had the skill of negotiating, be it with teachers or cooks in the mess of his hostel or anyone generally. Most of the time, he would offer me the lunch in the mess instead of the home-cooked lunch my mother packed for me. He thought he had been brilliant in this and I thought the same about myself.

But he was actually the smartest of the four of us. His confidence bagged him the job of a cricketing coach in a girls college. And soon enough he had the pretty president of the Students Union, Daljit Kaur riding pillion on a borrowed bike to watch 'Bobby' in Faridabad. The film had been released in the neighbouring towns before Delhi to give it the hype by the master showman Raj Kapoor.

We were content spending time in the Coffee Home and watching cricket matches in the Hindu College, munching peanuts. But even that was cut short abruptly.

One chilly morning in December as we were enjoying a match after class, a messenger came from her home to pick her up saying that her mother wanted her home urgently.

Two days later, she came back and announced that she had been engaged to an IPS officer from Allahabad, her home town.

I was shattered and heartbroken and helpless. Ajay came home in the evening, and we went to watch 'Achanak' by Gulzar to get over the shock. I Came back, wrote some teary poetry and had dinner.

That was the last I saw of Surekha. For almost 25 years we remained uncommunicative. I got married and changed many cities in the course of my job.

My last posting was in Bhopal when I got a call from Shashi that Surekha was in a hospital in my city. Locating her was not difficult. After being introduced to her husband, I learnt that Surekha was going to donate one of her kidneys to her estranged father, who was almost on his death-bed.

I rushed to her room. She had been put on the stretcher, and as she was being wheeled out to the OT, she hastily scribbled something on a piece of paper and held it out to me.

"I know you had read the Bhagavad Gita as a subject in philosophy in college. Please advise me whether I should act like Bheeshma or Krishna today," she pleaded with those familiar kajal-painted eyes which had enchanted me.

Yes, I had read the Gita and Krishna as the Charioteer of Arjun had inspired, rather instigated, a reluctant Arjun to pick up his bow and arrow and finish off his enemies who represented Adharma or evil. The Bhagavad Gita is an enunciation of his conversation with Arjun on the battle-field.

"Don't be blinded by your feelings. You have to finish off your enemies who have tormented you, without remorse," something like that.

Surekha had hinted many times how her estranged father had maltreated her mother and left them alone when they were growing up. Why should she be expected to donate her kidney to him just because he was her biological father? The doctors of course dutifully informed her that it was not a big deal as people could survive on one kidney as well as they did on two.

But if I am right the noblest character of Mahabharta is not Krishna but Bheeshma who was with the Kauravas knowing fully well that they were wrong, because he had made some commitments which were more important than his personal beliefs.

Krishna, on the other hand, had advised the Pandavas to practice deceit and cheating to beat the enemy when they were at their weakest. It would not be an exaggeration to say that 'All is Fair in Love and War' was a slogan that was propounded and practised by Krishna for the first time.

Would Krishna advise Surekha to give her kidney to her dying father as part of her Duty? Or would he tell her there is no brother, no father, no uncle, no no one in this war between Good and Evil and she should never forget what she and her mother had been made to go through?

I read the paper again and again and finally walked out of the hospital, leaving her to take that crucial decision. Even Krishna would have been at a loss to suggest her a course of action at that moment.

I never got to know what happened finally. Did the tormented quintessential Surekha succumb to her years of pent up anger and frustration or gave up her personal grievances to emulate the character she always wanted to follow - Mother Teresa, as I teasingly called her?

~~~trice of incubus - subjugation by a spirit~~~

Dulal had just joined the service at Haflong, before the raw tang of a college student had entirely dissipated, along with other colleagues on the same day after the completion of training together. Coincidentally they were all of the same age - young, tender, peppy and exuberant. But Dulal being a naturalist by hobby was enraptured by the pulchritude of the loan hill town in Assam, a quintessential example for real majestic, picturesque and aesthetic scenic view. But Dinu (Dinendra), his colleague and friend had the propensity of pulling his leg.

One day he caught hold of his personal diary and started reading loudly, "Nature has bestowed her orientation galore by embellishing with both hands a regal, paradisiacal and impeccable pulchritude and daintiness, which is by far the most naturally beautiful town, I have ever come across. A real treat for nature-lovers, for its enchanting, eye-popping and breathtaking views and a rare scenic elegance of lush green hilltop. The arcane Jatinga village, where ornithologists all over the world feel bamboozled regarding paradoxical mass nocturnal suicide by migratory birds, is hardly five KM away from Haflong. Jatinga mystery and inscrutable bird..."

Dulal snatched away his personal diary, "Don't dare touch it."

Bachchu Commented, "Very nicely depicted, awesome!"

At this Dinendra told, "What is nice here? What is there at Haflong, no life, no hustle-bustle? Monotonous life becomes standstill after 7 O'clock, as secluded as a graveyard."

Dulal strongly opposed, "What do you know about life? Life is best suited under nature & natural environment; it is ecology that will not pierce in your boulder head!" They continued ceaselessly when all others fled away.

It was a chilly, dusky, misty and delusory night at Haflong, when Dulal proposed, "We shall continue playing carom until some of us catch the sight of catnap and he will be penalized for next day's evening tea & snacks."

"Agreed your excellency," Dinu quipped. Playing carom in their recreation room usually from evening was more fun than recreation. At about 02:30 AM, Bachchu shouted, "Enough is enough, let us draw the curtain. For you useless guy I have constipation, the system is..." He did not complete.

After bidding goodbye to all his colleagues residing in a mess nearby office, Dulal all alone started for his residence, a KM away, at Ladies park, which is analogous to a delta surrounded on three sides by the majestic and sinuous Haflong lake, leaving small patches of land to integrate Ladies park (a hillock) by 164 steep stairs. The road was devoid of streetlights and utterly secluded. That night was extremely dark of the new moon. Furthermore, the dense fog made the night utterly murky.

"Oh! What a cracking hospitable welcoming home! I have eyes but of no use; I have all the moral hurry to reach home, being already late but I am ceaselessly conferred with a dim and dusky patch of darkness on my way of stepping. My foot knows not where I am putting it - land or water or anything else," Dulal murmured.

He was shambling, wobbling, on the road by the sides of meandering lake, failed thoroughly to descry the edge of the lake and was all but on the threshold of toppling down. He was waddling like a four-footed animal using two hands & feet to fend off tumbling into the lake. Eventually, he forestalled the jeopardy of toppling that night. Then he had to pass on a small wooden bridge, connecting the two sides of the lake. It was so pitch-dark that he could not surmise the entry to the bridge and was milling around. So he once again became four-footed, and using hands, he tried to perceive the existence of wood of the bridge, and finally his vague attempt became fruitful to ascend the bridge.

When he was halfway down the bridge, he sensed enigmatically amid that darkling jet black, something appeared darker, more caliginous and compact right in his face. He was on tenterhooks and asked himself,

"What it could be? A leopard or any other wild animal or preternatural creature!" All on a sudden in a lightning flash, he reminisced a narrative recounted by many inhabitants of Haflong, who had experienced an incredible witness of a widow in white Saree emerged out of the lake out of blue, up to an ever fruitless blackberry tree at the edge of the lake, again hurling herself down to the lake.

The tree was barely fifteen meters away, from where he was rooted to the ground. His heartbeat started pulsating faster & rapid - unbridled. He heard his own heartbeat, like the beating of multiples of drums at hundreds of decibels. A chill breeze surged around his spine. He started perspiring in such bitter cold. Dulal's heart was in his mouth; utterly spooked, petrified and got stuck. He was comprehensively clueless & thunderstruck, utterly became torpid, enervated and benumbed. He tried to budge his limbs, but futile. This haunted silent dormancy plagued for about seven harrowing minutes, and he could not even think of falling back as he had already crossed the Rubicon.

Suddenly out of desperate last-ditch, he plunged in risking - 'To hit or miss' - he tugged all his (fast diminishing) energy, vigour and resilience left, to recuperate equanimity & placidity, as 'desperate times call for desperate measures'. Slowly but steadily he retrieved his fortitude & quietude to some extent, though the heartbeat was bent upon to make him listen to her erratic and vexatious drum music coercively and he was equally unrelenting to ignore with all his might. He became wildly harum-scarum and stretched his hands to feel what it could be!? The instance that he extended his hands, he heard a shrill and explicit cry, "*O Baba go, Ma go, Bhuth, Bhuth* (Oh my father, Oh my mother, it's a ghost/spirit)", and scampered out of his sight in the twinkling of an eye.

Suddenly he rediscovered his full aplomb & tranquillity in contrast to his consternation a nanosecond hence. He stood tall and started walking slowly but steadily towards his destination, devoid of any qualm relieved from grisly incubus. He imbibed the lesson of his life that - 'Spirit is there. It dwells in our mind, especially when our enfeebled and succumbed mind is subjugated by certain prerequisites like a secluded place at night, cryptic darkness of night, misty & hallucinatory weather and all the more, the fictitious tales that we blindly inherit from our forefathers or friends.' Today he thinks, the situation could have easily been reversed had he not enough nerve up & became foolhardy at that terrifying moment and thus escaped from being a nincompoop by being reticent, when it matters most.

~~~amyra's first love: jeff & their startup~~~

Jeff Timmins' advertising business, Clare's Advertising had expanded manifolds, having bagged many prestigious contracts, and had almost gained the ranking of being the leading agency. From being a much talked about start-up to being considered as an agency of high repute and with major brands coming to them, Jeff felt on top of the world, but he had not forgotten his Amyra.

Joe, Tina, Sarah and Peter had all been promoted to higher ranks in the company. There was a staff of about 100 people, and they had moved to a bigger complex in South Mumbai.

There was a sudden flurry of activity in the IPO market, and companies were even listing their shares in the overseas stock exchanges. Jeff had singlehandedly taken Clare's to such great heights. The Hyderabad based Venture Capitalists had made an exit from the business and Jeff had approached investment bankers for the much-needed funds for expansion and to make an offer to the public.

Clare's Advertising was being valued at Rs 500 crore. Jeff was a happy man. At his new sprawling office on the 7th floor of Sky Heights building, Clare's was the only advertising agency office. The others were corporate offices of established food chains, and some were NGO Trusts and smaller offices.

One afternoon just after lunchtime, Jeff called Joe, Tina, Sarah and Peter to his cabin and said, "You all have contributed to the growth of the business. We are now a much bigger firm, and I have reached a stage where we can make an offer to the public. Isn't this a big milestone we have achieved? How would you like to celebrate? A rooftop party perhaps!"

From amongst the four of them, only Joe replied, "Ah… yes, we would like to celebrate this momentous occasion. A small gathering with a few close people will do, however. It needn't be that grand Jeff."

He looked surprised by that answer. "Okay! As you'll suggest. Please make a guest list and hand it over to me. I might want to add a few names, please."

The meeting got dispersed. In the meanwhile, Jeff had a couple of meetings with the bankers to finalize about the offer.

The business reports and the other expansion plans of the business were with Jeff in the pen drive. He called Sarah just before the bankers meeting and asked her to take the print outs and make a file. "I'll do this right away, Jeff."

The offer price for the shares was Rs 100 per share. There were shares of agencies listed in the US stock exchanges like Nasdaq and Dow Jones too early. But the main competition for Clare's Advertising was

BBDO and Synergy Advertising which had also gained a stronghold in the business.

The market was buzzing with the news of the IPO, and Jeff had to even make announcements to the media. He was waiting for an opportune time to make the news public. The IPO was to come out in the next couple of months. The other companies who were listed in a similar business were doing well, and share prices had also risen on the local indices.

Jeff did not want to miss out on the opportunity. He would be a majority shareholder with a few shares in Amyra's name as well. The IPO meant that Jeff was going to be the owner of a listed company, and there would be regular meetings in the office and also Annual General Meetings with the shareholders. He was feeling ecstatic.

The venture capitalists had sold their stake in the company, and Clare's had become one of the leading agencies in India. Jeff Timmins had reached a position that few could achieve in such a short period.

Amyra had quit the company after her wedding and Jeff had been missing his business partner. Amyra's childhood crush Rahul was head over heels about her. They had been married for nearly two years and had settled in Florida, USA. It was 2011, and Rahul did not stop surprising her with gifts every day. On some days he would bring the best of flowers which she would immediately place in the flower pot. Lilies and Orchids were her favourites. On some days he would bring expensive perfumes and satin dresses. She was happy with Rahul. One day while Rahul had been out of the house on work, she called Nancy and said, "Oh Nancy, why don't you visit us? I have lots of catching up to do. Rahul showers me with presents every other day!"

Nancy replied, "Of course Amyra and he rightly should. Yes, I will surely drop by for a month or so and spend time with you."

They soon decided to shift to Mumbai on Amyra's insistence. "I would like to be with daddy as well, Rahul. Can we please go back to Mumbai?"

Rahul had to yield to her request. And just a few days before their third wedding anniversary he booked tickets back to India.

"I hope you're happy now, my dear!"

"Oh yes, I'm so delighted Rahul. Can't wait to meet dad."

After their marriage, Rahul and Amyra stayed in Neptune Apartments which Rahul had recently purchased after moving to Mumbai. Amyra called their home 'Paradise'. His father, Gajanan was not staying with them. However, he did come to their house once in a while.

During one of his visits to Paradise, he took Rahul aside and said in a softer tone, "Looks like you two are well settled Rahul. Why don't you plan on adding a new member to the family?"

Rahul was not opposed to the idea at all. In fact, he was overjoyed at the thought of becoming a father. "Sure dad! I'll discuss this with Amyra. We need the blessings of our elders."

"We all are here for both of you son."

Amyra, at times, would just withdraw from Rahul and he was left clueless. He realized then that she might have been missing her mother. But she did not speak about it at all with him. She seemed to be quite happy. Rahul decided he would talk to her about having a baby. But he just did not how to bring out the topic.

One of the days in the morning when Amyra prepared the breakfast he decided he would speak to her. The two were seated on the breakfast table in the dining room. She had made Rahul's favourite Kanda Poha, fried egg and orange juice that day. It was about 10 in the morning, and the weather was lovely with a little bit of sunshine and the chirping of the birds outside.

"Can I have a word with you, honey?"

"Yes sure, what is it?" Said Amyra.

Rahul looked at Amyra lovingly. She stood there beside the table, waiting for a reply. He paused and then said, "My dear, don't you feel we should start a family. Now is a perfect time. Dad was here, and he agrees with me, my love."

Amyra promptly replied, "No, I don't think so! We need to first discuss other important things. I'm not okay with the idea of having a baby at this point in time." Rahul looked at her in disagreement. However, he refrained from getting into any argument with Amyra.

"We'll talk about it later when you're more receptive and understanding of me Amyra," Rahul said in a bit of an angry tone.

"Yes, sure when the other issues are addressed, I do not mind bringing up this topic," replied Amyra.

Amyra had lost her mother at a young age, and her father Shekhar was the sole person who stood by her in all the critical decisions she took in her life. Besides, Nancy, their housemaid being her very close confidant.

She got married to her childhood love Rahul with the blessings of Shekhar and Gajanan. But she always kept her mother's letters close to her and read them repeatedly whenever she felt sad or forlorn. She missed Neerja very much.

Post her wedding to Rahul there was something she was missing. Her work. And she was eager to return to Jeff's company, Clare's Advertising.

She once was a partner in the firm, and since she left post her marriage to Rahul, Clare's had expanded exponentially, and Jeff had taken the business to newer heights. The news was out that he would be launching an IPO soon.

Amyra read in the pink papers about Clare's, and she had made up her mind to rejoin the company at any cost. She missed the days when she and Jeff would spend long hours in the office working to bag the most prestigious contracts.

When Shekhar paid a visit to Paradise, Amyra became very emotional. Tears began to roll down her cheeks. "Oh father, you've come after so many months. I've been waiting to meet you. How is your health by the way?"

"I'm fine, my dear. I was just waiting for a good time to come here and speak to you," Shekhar promptly replied.

Rahul was at work. Amyra had informed him that dad would be coming home. He said he would try to come back early for dinner.

"I must join Clare's. Look where the company's reached. Jeff needs me. We started the company together, and I'm still a part of it."

"So this is what you wanted to discuss so urgently? I'm surprised by your decision, Amyra. You have a life with Rahul now. Aren't you planning to start a family? In fact, Gajanan and I were having a talk regarding the two of you just the other day."

If you think I'm going to say a yes to you for this, you're mistaken Amyra!

But dad, at least hear me completely!

Shekhar looked very upset and sighed, "Oh, how I was sceptical you would say this Amyra. I know both of you very well… Jeff will jump at the idea of having you back in his office. But you're a married woman now, you must remember that. And Rahul is your husband, and he might not approve of this. Work should not be more important than him for you."

Amyra interrupted him, "But dad." Shekhar continued, "Look Amyra, your mother would most definitely disagree to this, and let me make this known to you that I am unhappy about you being so adamant. Also, I need to be very sure that there's nothing more to this other than you working with Jeff."

Amyra looked into her dad's eyes to reassure him, "I wouldn't want to disappoint you. I love you and respect your opinion."

Rahul had been waiting to celebrate Amyra's 27th birthday. He had spent months preparing for the day. He loved her very much and never disagreed with her. Few months before her birthday on the 8th of October in 2012, he called her close beside him.

"My love, we will have a grand celebration for your birthday this year. Since we could not have a big celebration on your 26th birthday in the US, we shall have a grand party this year. I shall make sure that all invitations are sent out on time."

"Sure, Darling! I would love that! I have to make all the necessary preparations. And buy a nice dress. I've seen a lovely pink gown in the latest edition of the Vogue magazine, and I know where to buy it from," said Amyra in an excited tone.

Days passed, and invitations had gone to everyone. Both the families were also preparing for the big day to be celebrated at the banquet hall of The Pride Hotel located in the western suburbs.

Jeff would buy expensive gifts for Amyra on her birthday when they had been together. They were very much in love then. But now things were different.

While Jeff had still not forgotten her, he wondered how to send her the gift he had bought.

Through friends, he had come to know about the birthday celebrations, and he had decided he would go there himself to give her the presents.

At sharp 9 PM, he arrived in a grey suit with a bouquet of roses. His eyes searched for Amyra, and he knew that prettiest amongst them all would be her. After almost ten minutes of looking out for her, he spotted Amyra. She wore a burgundy one-piece dress with a lovely satin lace. Her hair was neatly done in a high bun.

Jeff went straight to her and wished her. Rahul wasn't around at that time. Amyra took the flowers from Jeff and thanked him.

"I hope you're not missing me at Clare's very much?"

Jeff stood there with a glass of red wine. He said in a soft tone, "Not as much as I had thought Amyra. A little more, I guess. But yes, I have managed to grow the business and have made sure we are in the top five list of agencies."

"I'm happy to hear that. I truly am," Amyra replied with a cute smile on her face.

"Is it also true that you're on the lookout for a suitable match for you? Can I be of some assistance Jeff?"

"Oh, no-no! That's not true. Some people just spread these rumours, you see. Don't you believe what you hear Amyra."

Amyra looked disappointed. "Oh! I wished it was true!" I think that you should settle down with someone."

Jeff just brushed aside the topic and said, "So any plans of joining work? Let me know if and when you do."

"Yes, sure I will let you know first the day I decide to join work. Who else would I ask beside you, Jeff?" Amyra whispered to Jeff.

"I'm aware that your dad's opinion would matter to you if you did so and I speak on your behalf if you so wish," continued Jeff.

Suddenly Rahul came looking for her as they were having this conversation and Jeff excused himself. She joined Rahul and cut the cake while all present cheered for them both.

Jeff had left the venue. He left in his Porsche and went home from the party.

~~~living the dream~~~

"Dear M, sometimes I feel like a drum without sound, a bird without wings and a diamond without its shine. I don't know who I am and often find myself doing all the wrong things at all the right times. Caught up in the wrong job, you see? And quitting doesn't seem to be the best option as I am too scared to face the question of 'what next'? I am not able to find out that is it my boss or my company or my job profile because of which I want to resign. Guess it's a mixture of all. Wish I could just sing the song *'Main chahe ye karu, main chahe wo karu, meri marzi…'* and dodge all the questions and answers. How do I make my not so happening work-life so-called perfect and exciting?

Yours Misfit."

After reading this query in a popular fashion magazine Agony Hour's column, I suddenly felt as if it is me asking the same question. Oh well, let me introduce myself. I am Simran Sabarwal or Simmy, a bubbly, witty, intelligent, imaginative & unapologetic girl who wants everything in life. Well, everything includes hottest of dresses, coolest of friends, biggest of parties, yummiest of food & a prince charming. Does it sound too much? Not to me at least.

God and I are best friends, although our plans rarely match. I always wanted to go to a creative field like dancing, but destiny had some other plans for me. I am now working with a major consulting MNC in the HR department, rendering them operational support. In layman terms, *'files / records bana ke rakhti hun yaar.'*

If you ask me what your favourite dish is, I would say Excel; if you ask me how many boyfriends you have, I would say tracker, charts, tables and not to forget a Dell notebook. My life is nothing over the top or out of the box.

The only unique thing that I have is my family that has my Mom (*1970s ki Miss Kapurthala*), my Dadi (a modernized version of Nirupa Roy), Dad (who resembles one of the Prisoners from Azkaban) and a brother who thinks of himself as Sonu Nigam but is nothing better than a pirated version of Himesh Reshammiya. We are all four different pillars supporting a single wall with a slogan 'we are family.'

I have always done things *hatke*. As all my friends in group would take part in sports & I would be the one going for cooking classes or my entire family would go for ice cream and I will sit near a *chai-wala* and have *chai*. So you get what I mean when I say *hatke*, right? But as it is said that sometimes it just takes a single moment to change your life. That moment could be a moment of fun, moment of luck or moment of decision (like mine).

It was a very bright sunny day of summer with the sun being in its full spirits and me in my dullest of moods going to the office. I had got a good dose of the so-called extended conversation from my supervisor on a miss that I happened to make related to my work. I generally don't hold on to such conversations much but this one I just could not let go off as it seemed to wither away the difference between being rude and being disrespectful. I was constantly thinking about it as I was going to board my cab. It was for the first time I did not feel like entering the premises of my office as if something inside me was stopping me from doing it. But I did eventually. I did not wish anyone good morning and sat on my seat and opened my laptop.

Just then my phone rang. I said "Hello. Who is this?" in a very monotonous tone and the reply came as "*Hello moti …kaisi hai.*" I immediately recognized the voice, it was my best friend Ria on the other side. Her call kind of woke me up & I was glad to hear her voice after a long time. But suddenly after a second when I was over with my gladness I felt that her voice sounded much lower than mine & I could not stop myself from asking what had happened. Ria had met with a terrible road accident and underwent a major spinal cord surgery a month back.

I wanted to go and meet her but she being in Kolkata and me in Mumbai, made it practically impossible. I wanted to ask her when, how, where etc. but I did not want to upset her more by reminding her of the event once again, so I started off casually by saying "hope you are doing good now & wish u a speedy recovery." Numerous thoughts were going in Ria's mind, and she wanted to speak about it to someone and who is better than a childhood best friend. Ria was working with one of the most significant manufacturing MNC as an Assistant Manager - finance. She was always those *munshi ji* types who loved accounts and mathematics; hence her choice of career was quite evident. We used to hang out together in childhood, eat, play & even sleep together sometimes. We shared a passion for dancing and also went to the dance classes along and were the top performers in school as well.

While we were running down the memory lane just then Ria started crying on the phone. When I asked her if her wound was hurting the reply was even further painful. She told me that due to her spinal cord operation, she will never be able to dance. All this hale when she was working in the corporate world, she could never give time to herself and her hobbies. It was always meetings, the offsite community meets, deadlines, schedules etc. She never missed dancing but only realized the importance of it in her life when she was told she will never be able to dance. And the very reason for her call that day was to say to me that life is too short and we must do what we want to and not what life makes us do. She knew that I always inhibited a secret ambition of becoming a choreographer one day and open my own dancing school and teach poor kids.

She made me realize that while working on fulfilling the basic needs of our body like food, clothes etc. we often forget to feed our heart and soul and do things which can only make us happy temporarily but do not lead us to self-contentment and satisfaction and inner joy. While I was listening to each and every word of her carefully, somewhere, my mind and heart had already made a decision. I did not even realize that it had been 40 minutes that we were chatting. I quickly wished her speedy recovery and thanked her for calling me and disconnected the call with a promise of meeting her soon.

Just then I went to my workstation and opened my laptop and clicked on the 'new mail' icon and started typing…

'Dear xxx,

Kindly accept this mail as a formal notice of my resignation from xxx, and I intend to be relieved from my services from today itself. Will make sure that I close all my exit formalities today itself and the notice period can be deducted from my monthly payout as per the company policy. Thank you once again for all the support.

Thanks & Regards,

Simran'

After typing this letter, suddenly a sense of relief and joy prevailed over my mind and heart. Everything seemed to become clear, and I felt much more confident. And the rest was history. Needless to say that the day went ahead with long discussions and exit interviews, but in the end, I was relieved from my services the very day itself.

Then came the question of 'what next?' which I was dreaded the most but this time the new & confident me did not let me loose. I always wanted to go to Terrance dance school and officially learn contemporary style dancing. Surprisingly when I told my parents about my resignation, they did not react at all as they were aware of the dissatisfaction piling up in me since quite some time. They were very supportive and allowed me to choose and live the life I wanted to. I immediately took the address from Terrance dance academy official website and went to their office the next day morning and enrolled myself. I learnt and was trained by a very professional set of instructors.

After a good one year, my dad became severely ill, and I had to go back to my hometown. All seemed to be over, but my mother told me not to give up, and I opened my own dance school in my hometown at a tiny scale. I had five students initially for a month or so with a very meagre fee of Rs 500 per month. Slowly and steadily as people came to know about the classes and the positive word of mouth from my students the number of enrolments rose to 20 and then 30 and then after three months I had a total strength of 50 students in my classes, and I called them my 'Fantabulous 50'. The fee that came from my classes was just enough for my dad's medicine and other household expenses.

Then one day, a student came to me with a pamphlet of a group dance competition by the name of 'Entertainer of the year.' It was a ray of hope for me. The prize money for the winning team was 25 lakh rupees. I was thrilled to see that, but at the same time, knew it would be difficult. Just when I was thinking, my students just played the song *'Tu naa jaane aas paas hai khuda...'* and started dancing on it and again that very moment of my life made me take the decision of participating in the competition. I practised with my entire group for a month as the auditions were after a month. Life surprisingly started giving way to whatever I was thinking. We cleared the initial selection round followed by two contesting rounds and a semi-finals.

Then came the Day of Judgment, 'The Grand Finale.' As an instructor, I was supposed to encourage my group, but I just told them all the best and went on the terrace for some time alone where my heart was speaking to my mind. Strangely some very prominent quotes that I had come across at some point of my life just started floating in front of my eyes and humming in my ears.

"Your time is limited, so don't waste it living someone else's life. Don't be trapped by dogma - which is living with the results of other people's thinking. Don't let the noise of others' opinions drown out your own inner voice. And most important, have the courage to follow your heart and intuition." - Steve jobs

You must never doubt your ability to achieve anything, become anything, overcome anything and inspire everything.

And at last, my own mantra that I always follow, 'do your best, God will do the rest.' I took a deep breath and said, "bring it on baby!" and went down for the final show. My group performed like there is no tomorrow and had the best time of our life. And when the winner was announced, everything seemed to have become still for a while, and there was absolute silence. All I could hear was a complete vacuum in the background and bright light in front of my eyes. Moments later, tears started flowing from my eyes with a big smile on my face. Everything was weird but wonderful.

In the end, I had achieved what I aimed at, and today after 10 years when I look back, I have so much to relish. I have my dance classes franchisees in the biggest four metros in India where we teach to kids who not only love dancing but love and dare to live their dancing dream.

~~~is it superstition or reality?~~~

The story is set in Delhi. Khyati Arora hails from a middle-class family, residing in a society with her family. She is the single child of her parents. Her father is a government official, working in one of the prominent ministries while her mother (a medical lab technician) is working in an MCD Hospital. Since 8th grade, she had dreamt of pursuing Journalism and Mass Communication. Even though she had cleared all the entrances, she finally settled for BJMC as this was her chance to go ahead with her passion.

April 2011

It was her first day of college. She woke up early and went to the nearby temple. She gets dressed and opts to put on a black t-shirt and blue denim with black sneakers. She looked at herself one last time in the mirror before leaving. Though it was a 15-minute ride from her home, she preferred to go with auto-rickshaw. She was lucky enough to find one as soon as she reached the main road.

Driver: *Kahan jana hai madam?* (Where do you want to go, madam?)

Khyati: VIPS College. *Kya ap chaloge?* (Will you go?)

Driver: *Hanji madam. 50 lagenge.* (Yes, madam. It will be 50 rupees.)

While the auto drove, her mind was filled with various thoughts. She was excited yet nervous. Her train of thoughts broke when the rickshaw halted at the red light. It was a brief stop, but for her, it felt like hours. She unlocked her phone to check the time. 9:30 A.M. the clock showed. Just then, she was startled with a masculine voice.

"*Aye didi* (while clapping hands). *Aye didi, bhagwan apko sukhi rakhe, main apke lie dua karegi.* (I will pray for you, may you always be happy)." She said while placing her hand on Khyati's head to give her blessings. She was a third gender (*kinnar*) dressed in a bright orange saree with red lipstick, eyes lined with kohl and a big red bindi on her forehead.

Khyati always had a soft corner for them. Call it coincidence or her fondness for them, that she had never let them go empty-handed. She believed in the notion which every Indian has about the third gender. That they have psychic powers and their presence and blessings are considered to be prosperous, and their curse is all the more catastrophic.

Khyati searched for change in her handbag and quickly found a 20 rupee note. She happily handed it to the eunuch.

With a broad smile on her face, the eunuch blessed her and said, *"Bhagwan apko humesha sukhi rahenge, phalo phulo, khoob tarakki karo sundar didi."* (May God always bestows you with happiness and success, my beautiful sister).

Even before Khyati could thank her, she swiftly moved to the car standing beside her auto to try if she could get some cash. Khyati felt lucky enough that on her first day, she was blessed with the eunuch's wishes. As for the rest of the journey, her mind was filled with the flashbacks of the encounters she had with them till now.

The auto driver suddenly said, *"Madam, Inhe mat dia karo paise. Ye log bas yahi karte hain. Aur kuch toh hote bhi nhi hain tab bhi ban jate hain kyun ki kamana nahi chahte."*

(Ma'am, you shouldn't give them money as they are greedy. Some of them are not even legit transgender. They just don't want to work and earn money respectfully).

"Bhaiya, mera iraada toh acha tha na. Ye unke karam hain ki wo kis roop mein ban ke paise le rahe hain ya uss paise ka kya kar rahe hain. Bas mera vishwaas hai inn pe isliye main de deti hu. Aisa lagta hai inki dua aur aashirwaad mere lie kaam kr jati hain."

(My intent is good. It is their karma as in which way they pose themselves to mint money or what they do with that money. When they bless me, I believe their wishes bring me luck).

An Indian at various points in his/her life has seen the third gender at their place or around them. It's like they have either a strong network or telepathic vibes, that whenever someone in the family gets married or has a kid, they come over with their troupe. Dressed up in bright sarees, adorned with jewellery and makeup, they sing and dance merrily and extend their blessings and love to the family. In return, they expect to be given a considerable amount of cash (which is known as sagan or shagun in India). Khyati had seen them thrice at her place on the day of her aunt's and cousin's wedding and when a close cousin was born.

While their presence and blessing are considered to be auspicious, people maintain a safe distance from them. Some even exploit and harass them. They have been marginalized and discriminated against by society. They are not given equal opportunities and have to struggle for two square meals a day.

For Khyati, that day and the coming days in the college went fantastic. She went on to make some amazing friends, was loved by both her faculty and batch mates and even excelled at her exams. Deep inside her heart, she owed it to that special person she met a few months back at the red light.

June 2014

She wrapped up her graduation with good marks. She was occupied with her post-graduation diploma entrances. The most important one was on the day of her birthday, 8th June. She was on a bus, on her way to the exam. She was studying when a eunuch approached her and requested for money. She scouted her bag for change but couldn't find any. She was able to get only a two rupee coin and was disappointed and upset.

The eunuch sensed that she was short of cash and was preparing for an exam. She took that coin from Khyati's hand and blessed her, "All the best for your exam. I wish you secure admission and may you succeed in life," she said and got down at the next stop.

Khyati was very emotional and shocked. The eunuch was not only educated but observant too as she noticed the entrance preparatory book. Khyati was on the seventh heaven. It was her birthday and as fate wanted it, on her special day she was blessed by a eunuch when she was for the first time short on money. All the rumours she had heard about them being greedy turned out to be false, at least for her. She silently prayed for the well-being of all the eunuchs in her heart.

After two months of that incident, she cleared the entrance and got admission to one of the most reputed colleges. She gives the credit for it to the eunuch she met that day while going for her exam.

October 2015

After completing her post-graduation diploma with flying colours, she was applying for jobs and was giving interviews. Since she had free time; she was on a cleaning spree. She started with her 'mini library'. It was a term she had given to a shelf in her cupboard dedicated to her collections of books. Well, a rack would sound small to some people, but for her being in a middle-class family, where one barely has extra space, this was a luxury for her! To have an area dedicated to just her love, her books. She emptied the shelf and cleaned it up. Whenever she did that, it was her habit that she would open every book, brush through its pages and soak in their smell. She was doing just the same when she picked up a book with a colourful cover and a catchy title, Almost Single, written by Advaita Kala. It was special not just because of the author but because it was a gift from someone special.

She went into a flashback that took her a year ago. She had just come back after her lectures and was resting when her mother entered the room. She had a book in her hand which she handed to Khyati and said,

"You remember Karan, the third gender, I mentioned about who keeps visiting me in the hospital?"

"Yes, Maa. I do remember. It is such a great thing that he is independent and has a partner, Rahul. Despite having his share of struggles, he is working and leading a healthy life."

"Yes, he works in a printing press and has given this book for you. He checked with me about this the last time he came for his tests. He probably thought I wouldn't take it because people usually are apprehensive about interacting with them. I told him that we respect them for who they are, what they wish to do and how they wish to identify. He was quite impressed. He had no idea that you love books, but his instinct made him offer one. So, this time when he came, he brought this book for you."

"That is so thoughtful of him. It's indeed a blessing in disguise for me and well, destiny too. I will always keep it with me."

'Dear Garima,
All the best!
May that smile never fade away.'

She read the message Karan had written and flipped through the pages. She felt the book was her lucky charm. Whenever tensed or upset, she would read it even though she had learned the lines by heart (because of the constant re-reading). She somehow felt the book had Karan's blessings and love. The book was her constant in this social media world and always healed and supported her.

Two weeks later, she got a job offer from one of the reputed Public Relations agencies of India. Her joy knew no bounds. She probably felt that going through the book two weeks back had worked wonders. The book had worked its magic that she landed up with that job.

2020

Khyati worked in the agency for three years. Her work was highly acknowledged and appreciated. All was good until, in January 2019, she fell seriously ill. She had to be hospitalized and was in ICU for five days, followed by 15 days in the ward. The doctors even though trying their best, had given up all hope. She had to struggle a lot. Too weak to move normally (even walking with support and sitting needed great efforts), 30 pills a day, lifesaving drugs, hair and weight loss, dark skin, five units of blood, countless drips, a point came when the doctors suspected cancer too. But the reports finally stated tuberculosis.

An independent, social 26-year-old girl was confined within the four walls of her room when it was her age to go out and have fun. Constant pain in the body, joints, and back made living life a tough task.

However, it took her a year and a half of patience, will power and courage to go through this tough time. Presently, she is tuberculosis free but is still facing some issues and is trying to get her normal life back, which will, of course, take time. But she is sure that she got this second life not only because of her will power, prayers of her family and friends but also because of the blessings of Karan.

Khyati feels that Karan was a significant reason for her survival. Call it coincidence or pure destiny that she always has their presence around her when she is about to embark on a new journey in life or has any trouble. Khyati wishes to do something valuable and contribute to their empowerment and upliftment in the society. For now, she is already in touch with the NGO's working for this same cause and is keen to be associated with them.

know more
about
our authors

~~~ravi dhar~~~

A native of Kashmir, India, Ravi Dhar has been a part of the Kashmiri Pundit Diaspora, since the age of ten, when he left the valley to study in a public school at Jammu. A postgraduate in English from the University of Jammu, Jammu, India, he earned his doctoral degree in English from the North-Eastern Hill University, Shillong, India. Ever since, he has been outside his native state, teaching in various Indian universities in India and the Ethiopian Civil Services College, Addis Ababa. He has traveled to Netherlands, Germany, Austria, Hungary, Czech Republic, Slovakia, Korea, Singapore, Malaysia, Thailand, Ethiopia and Sweden. Presently, he is Professor of Mass Communication at Jagannath International Management School, Vasant Kunj, New Delhi, India, of which he also happens to be the Director.

He has been editing an international journal of communication Studies, Mass Communicator, for the last four years. He has come out with an edited book on *Indian Management: Theory and Practice* and another book on *Global Perspectives on Media in the Swirl* is in press. He is also a poet, having published poems in *The Chant of Vitasta*. He has also published a novel titled *Orphans of the Storm*. A keen student of Indian philosophy and Integral Yoga, he believes in the creative evolution of humankind, an enlightened faith that he has inherited from his Guru, Sri Aurobindo/the Mother.

'The Mystical Break-in' is his creation. Ravi can be reached at ravikdhar@gmail.com

~~~shagun marwah~~~

Born and raised in the suburbs of New Delhi, India, Shagun Marwah is a writer by heart and an editor by profession. She has been weaving stories since she was 10 years old on almost everything and anything that fuels her interest and gives wings to her imagination.

After completing her schooling from Carmel Convent and graduation from Delhi University, she began her career with distinguished brands like Vogue, Conde Nast, and POPxo, only to realize thereafter that her true passion lies in fiction stories more than features on lifestyle and beauty. She loves being an editor for it gives her an opportunity to read unlimited novels penned down by different authors, which in their own ways, teach her something new each day. Funnily enough, her fondness for reading books as a child began with R. L. Stine's Goosebumps and till date, she finds herself drawn towards the horror genre section of a bookstore, reaching for the most gripping of thrillers.

When she's not writing, editing, or reading, she's probably watching horror/thrillers (the darker, the better) and romantic comedies (extreme polar interests for reasons unknown), devouring chicken momos (anything with chicken, really), or contemplating a quote she read somewhere with a strong cup of coffee. She aspires to be a novelist someday on a genre she wishes to keep a secret (or suspense!) - for now.

'The Value of a Claddagh' & 'We Hit the Jackpot!' are her creations. Shagun can be reached at shagunmarwah96@gmail.com

~~~lovey chaudhary~~~

Lovey Chaudhary is a Canada-based blogger, author and part time corporate slave. She has a blog which is called *Femonomic.* She authored a poetry book known as *Femonomic.* If that's not enough, she has other profiles on social media under the *Femonomic* label. The blog, the book, and social media accounts talk about only one thing, the freedom to have a conversation about anything and everything in the right way.

She started writing about world nuisances in college, and has written over 400 articles, 21 research papers, and changed four jobs to keep up with her passion for raw, dark, and uncanny writing.

Lovey writes satirically about social issues as that is the best she knows. She aims to publish 20 books under the same name, rightly you guessed, *Femonomic.* You can visit her website femonomic.com

'The Brutality of Reality' is her creation. Lovey can be reached at femonomic@gmail.com

~~~tapas chanda~~~

A former banker, Tapas Chanda (alias N.K Chanda) resides in Kolkata. He's a voracious reader and writing has been his forte from his school days. Chanda has already published several articles, essays and short stories across several platforms including newspapers and magazines. However, with a bank job, he couldn't dedicate much time for writing. So currently, he's working on a series of short stories inspired by the idiosyncrasies of our times.

Born in a small town in Assam, he's also penning his autobiography. The son of a Railway Station Manager, he has travelled extensively during his childhood and also as a banker.

An extrovert by nature, with a friendly disposition, he is a profound lover of classical music and English literature in which he has a deep understanding. He is a passionate reader of English literature and has an excellent command over it. Tapas has been residing in Kolkata for thirty years with his wife, daughter and son.

'Teeth in Love' is his creation. Tapas can be reached at chandanarendrasbi@gmail.com

~~~sriraka mazumder~~~

Sriraka Mazumder is a Senior Development Editor, English Education, Cambridge University Press. She strategizes and designs English courses for schools. She has over ten years of editorial experience in various sectors like print and digital publishing with schoolbooks, newspapers and magazines.

She hails from Kolkata and is now settled in Delhi. She has an eclectic range of hobbies - from studying literature and language to visual arts and performing arts. She has translated several stories from Bangla to English, including short stories from *Thakurmar Jhuli*, a collection of folklores from Bengal. She started writing from the age of six, and hasn't stopped ever since.

Sriraka believes in infusing fun in whatever she does, and lives by what a wise man had once said: Life would be tragic if it weren't funny.

'The Letter', 'Riju' & 'The Answer' are her creations. Sriraka can be reached at sriraka@gmail.com

~~~enakshi johri~~~

Enakshi Johri is an educator, author and traveller. Her writings have appeared in *The Speaking Tree (newspaper), Woman's Era, Alive, Infinithoughts, Sivana Spirit, Women's Web, efiction India and IndusWomanWriting*. Her stories and poems have been anthologized widely. She writes a weekly editorial, Odds and Evens, for a Social Journalism platform called *Different Truths*. She is also an eminent book reviewer and has been reviewing books for Penguin, Rupa, Hachette India and Half-Baked Beans for more than half a decade. She has conceptualized and edited two books - *Unbounded Trajectories* and *Poison Ivy* and is currently editing a third book called Cryptic Encounters.

She won the Most Influential Woman Award in 2020 organized by The Spirit Mania. She has been featured by Kalaage, Bibliophiles of Bangalore and Indibloghub. She posts articles, essays, poetry and reviews on her website, aliveshadow.com

'Blind Luck' is her creation. Enakshi can be reached at ejblog12@gmail.com

~~~jhelum~~~

Born and brought up in Calcutta, Jhelum, was infused with an aesthetic sense early on, with mother in beauty business and father in photography. In addition, her city made her a bibliophile, and later she pursued her M.A. and M.Phil in English Literature from Jawaharlal Nehru University.

A dreamy lover of Keats's poetry, she did not want to turn into a critic from an incorrigible Romantic, which is what academic profession requires. So she decided to tap into her heritage, and joined the India Today group and worked as a beauty editor for a decade for lifestyle magazines like Harper's Bazaar, Good Housekeeping and Women's Health. Thereafter, she took up the role of the marketing head for Sephora India.

In 2014, Jhelum had to take a sabbatical from work due to ill health. However, this proved to be a boon. As she healed herself with alternative therapies, she began learning them as well. She started a website on beauty, beautybeats.in and created a collection of beauty products called Jhelum Loves.

Recently she has written a book 'Phoolproof: Indian Flowers, Their Myths, Traditions & Usage', published by Penguin Random House. She continues to contribute articles in various lifestyle magazines, and also writes poems and short stories. In 2019 she moved to Bangalore, and now divides her time between three cities - Kolkata, Delhi and Bangalore, surrounded by fairies, flowers, friends, family and some other animals.

'Cafuné', 'Saudade' & 'Petrichor' are her creations. Jhelum can be reached at jhelum@beautybeats.in

~~~hasina saiyeda~~~

Hasina Saiyeda is a Kolkata-based content writer who has a knack of telling stories to the world. She loves writing and contributes to blogs and other online platforms. Being passionate about writing she took it up as a profession and targets to share her ideas with larger audience. She writes in simple English so that everyone can read her stories. Her debut novel is 'Passion VS Parents… the game is on'.

'Vibhatsu - the deathly fear' is her creation. Hasina can be reached at hasina.saiyeda@gmail.com

~~~sukriti malik~~~

Sukriti is an exception to this anthology. While contributors to this book are highly accomplished individuals and have done significant work in their fields, Sukriti is new to writing.

Her story in this book is her first-ever published work. Despite completing it in less than four hours, she thinks of herself of an ordinary calibre - a person so humble that when asked for a bio for the book, got nervous and could not think of anything.

She resides in Delhi and currently studying management. She also possesses a balanced blend of modern and old school thoughts, that when needed, help her easily break the conventions.

Being a nature lover, she likes gazing at the night sky. She is meditative by temperament & draws inspiration from her family.

'The Last Leaf' is her creation. Sukriti can be reached at maliksukriti1@gmail.com

~~~suchismita ghoshal~~~

Co-authoring for more than 150 anthologies, journals & magazines, both from national and international arenas, Suchismita Ghoshal from Malda, West Bengal dreams high to achieve the heights keeping her feet to the ground. Being a science graduate, currently majoring in Political Science and pursuing a diploma in Media Science and Mass Communication, she also works as a social activist for a Govt. Registered NGO 'Prayas Welfare Society'.

A poet, professional writer, scribbler, professional book critic, storyteller, columnist, copy-editor at Notion Press Publishing, content writer, creative writing professional, nature lover and a change agent and a position holder as Worldwide Ambassadors' Coordinator for Global Youth Leaders Network, Suchismita also aims to heal people with the majesty of her words.

She is also an environmental activist who recently brought reality to her dream as her debut book named 'Fields of Sonnet'. Her hard work has decorated her with several awards and accolades till now including Rex Karmaveer Chakra Award (instituted by iCONGO and powered by United Nations), Author Pages Best Woman Writer Award 2020, Indian Youth Genius Award 2020, Indian Youth Star Awards 2020, Aaghaaz 2K20 Award, The Spirit Mania Influential Women Award 2K20, Top 50 Popular Author Awards 2K20 By The Spirit Mania and NE8X Literary Award 2K20.

'Troubled' is her creation. Suchismita can be reached at ghoshalsuchismita019@gmail.com

~~~amitabh srivastava~~~

Amitabh Srivastava is a Delhi based senior journalist and social sector expert. He has worked with top media platforms such as The Hindustan Times, Sahara Times, Saptahik Hindustan, Dinman, Patriot, Navjivan, National Herald etc. in a career spanning over four decades. His long association with NGO Prayas has given him close and deep insights into issues of children and women.

'So What?' is his creation. Amitabh can be reached at amitabh06@gmail.com

~~~sulay kumar chanda~~~

Sulay Kumar Chanda born in small town of Lumdimg in Assam, was brought up and groomed in Haflong. He completed his education and spent inceptive period of service at an aesthetic, picturesque, scenic beautiful Haflong.

He is a retired Telecom executive, retired on VRS from BSNL in March of 2020. From the childhood he had an acute and keen passion in reading storybooks, novels, any articles published in contemporary period. Being very introvert in nature, he never dreamt of writing himself until last few months. Inspired by his elder brother, who has a vast experience in writing, he took up pen. So he may be called a neophyte in the field of creativity. Nevertheless, he had ample experience in life, where queer and eerie incidents occasioned more than habitual and natural events which are not only thrilling but breathtaking.

A few of his stories have been published in esteemed Newspaper of Assam. He resides at Guwahati and is settled there.

'Trice of Incubus - Subjugation by a Spirit' is his creation. Sulay can be reached at sulay60@gmail.com

~~~divya jain~~~

Divya Jain, a commerce graduate from Narsee Monjee College of Commerce & Economics (Mumbai) pursued post-graduation from Kalina University in 2002 in Economics and Political Science. With a degree in Journalism from K C College she has had the privilege of working in leading newspapers like The Asian Age and The Financial Express and TV channels (Zee News) as a Correspondent.

An avid reader of renowned authors like J K Rowling, Agatha Christie, Jane Austen, John Green - Divya is also an artist and a blogger.

She is a published author and her debut novel *Love v/s Betrayal* was published in June 2017 by the Wordit Art Fund of Become Shakespeare. She has been interviewed by Book Thela, an online portal for book lovers and few youth magazines.

Besides, she has participated in several writing competitions. Her work was also selected by the Jaipur Literature Festival and was awarded a certificate by Jaipur Book Mark, for having taken part in the iwrite Cohort 2019.

'Amyra's First Love: Jeff and Their Start-up' is her creation. Divya can be reached at jain.24.divya@gmail.com

~~~richa rudra~~~

When asked about herself, Richa Rudra gave us the most bizarre answer we have ever received till now. At first, we thought she is kidding and would give us her bio as per convention. You know, a proper introduction of an author, their works and achievements etc.? Like all authors want to see in a book. However, she remained adamant and never changed her statement viz. "Well, I am crazy and work in progress."

'Living the Dream' is her creation. Richa can be reached at richarudra1@gmail.com (email her at your own risk!)

~~~garima batra~~~

Garima Batra resides in Delhi. She studied journalism and mass communication and has a post-graduation diploma in Public Relations. She has worked in the PR industry for close to three years.

Presently, she is on a sabbatical and exploring new opportunities in content writing. As for her hobbies, she likes to dance, read novels, indulge in DIY art and craft and is a travel buff. She loves to explore new places and possesses a love for French language. She loves to meet new people and make connections. She aspires to be a full-time writer and hopes to strike off this desire from her bucket list soon.

'Is it Superstition or Reality?' is her creation. Garima can be reached at bgarima08@gmail.com

~~~acknowledgements~~~

I take this opportunity to thank and congratulate all our contributors who made this book possible.

I also thank all those who showed interest in publishing with us but couldn't make it this time. We hope to work with you in the future.

Thank you! Dr Ravi Dhar, for withdrawing time upon our request to write for this anthology.

Finally, I would like to thank all our readers and authors for their love and support and for motivating us to keep doing what we do at Think Tank Books.

Gaurav Sharma
Editor - 'none of a kind'
Publisher - Think Tank Books